A Lig
Inclu

POOK SAHIB

Lieutenant Pook sounds pretty good, at least it did to Pook himself, who was seconded to the Royal Ramsami Navy to undertake the strangest mission ever to befall a naval officer. Precisely what that mission was, though, Pook never quite discovered.

Assisted by Honners as navigating officer, Peter Pook sets out from the Eastern state of Ramsam as crack naval diver of the Fleet, on board the mystery ship Soonong. In command of the vessel is one of the toughest characters ever to sail the notorious China Coast, Commander Bray - 250lb of the liverish breed that made Britain great, whose brilliant seamanship has made his name a legend throughout the repair yards of the Orient. His dislike of Pook is apparent from the first, and is helped along by jealousy over a beautiful half-caste girl, whom Pook unwittingly introduces to a house of ill-fame in the wicked city of Shaggapore.

With superb confidence, born of utter incompetence, Pook blunders through the hazards of naval diving, religious taboos and Oriental marriage, under the all-seeing eye of the Nawab of Ramsam. He flirts with the Nawab's wife, falls in love with a night-club singer, swims across a sacred lake and finally becomes enmeshed in the macabre religious practices of the Ramsamis.

Nevertheless he still finds time to be shipwrecked in the Bay of Bengal and sink a warship under his captain's feet. Happily, Commander Bray and Lieutenant Pook decide to bury the past like true shipmates and as a result of this resolve their bloody fight on the waterfront of Chattoo dockland sets a new standard in human conflict and endurance, albeit a new low in naval discipline. Whether or not the reader is acquainted with Pook's earlier adventures in *Banking on Form*, *Pook in Boots* and *Pook in Business,* he will recognize this personality as the funniest on the current comedy scene.

Also by Peter Pook:

Banking on Form
Pook in Boots
Pook in Business
Bwana Pook
Professor Pook
Banker Pook Confesses
Pook at College
Pook's Tender Years
Pook and Partners
Playboy Pook
Pook's Class War
Pook's Tale of Woo
Pook's Eastern Promise
Beau Pook Proposes
Pook's Tours
The Teacher's Hand-Pook
Gigolo Pook
Pook's Love Nest
Pook Omnibus
Pook's China Doll
Pook's Curiosity Shop
Marine Pook Esquire
Pook's Viking Virgins

PETER POOK

POOK SAHIB

A Light Satire On All Things Eastern
Including The English Who Go There

EMISSARY PUBLISHING
P.O. Box 33, Murdock Road,
Bicester, Oxon,, OX6 7PP, England.

First published in Great Britain 1965 by
Robert Hale Ltd.
Published in Omnibus 1976.

This edition published 1993 by
Emissary Publishing, P.O. Box 33, Murdock Road,
Bicester, Oxon., OX6 7PP.

British Library Cataloguing-in-Publication Data.
A catalogue record for this book is available from the British Library.

ISBN 1-874490-09-0

© Peter Pook 1965

This book may not be reproduced, in whole or in part, in any form (except by reviewers for the public press), without written permission from the copyright owner.

Printed in Great Britain by Manuscript ReSearch, Oxfordshire.

To all my good friends east of Suez, in the hope that they will smile once more at the bumptious character portrayed within - whom they treated with such good humour, long-suffering patience and lavish hospitality.

ONE

"We're rolling into Shaggapore Station, Peter," Honners cries delightedly. "Just think of it - you're actually in Shaggapore at last!"

I think about Shaggapore and try to appear excited, but fail miserably. The pleasure of meeting Honners again after so long has worn thin during the endless train journey from Naval Headquarters at Jawanagar through the ancient State of Ramsam. At the moment it does not feel so much like the completion of a journey as that I am being pensioned off after a lifetime on the railways.

I little suspect that ahead of me lies one of the most mysterious epics of the war - so secret that even today I am not permitted to reveal how we came to be involved in this classic maritime adventure conducted by the landlocked State of Ramsam, and disclosed here for the very first time. Himself sworn to secrecy, Honners has hinted that yet another British officer may be connected with the assignment - none other than Commander Bray, late of the Merchant Service, whose brilliant seamanship is already a legend throughout the repair yards of the East.

Link that illustrious name with Honners as Navigating Officer, and myself as crack diver of the Fleet, and you have a trio which prompted the *Ramsami Intelligence* to observe that such a formidable combination is sufficient to strike fear into the hearts of friend and foe alike.

At Shaggapore Terminus we are met by several Ramsami Rail Transport Officers who are obviously delighted to have a train to fuss over. They warn us that the Commodore of the Navy is waiting to greet us. His title is Commodore Gooji, and we espy him afar surrounded by his aide-de-camp and retinue. Honners informs me that a Commodore is entitled to a staff of thirty subordinates whose official designations sound like brand names of detergent powders.

The chief R.T.O. performs the elaborate introduction ritual, without which it is impossible to meet anybody in Ramsam. Hence we are all saluting and salaaming as though we have nervous tics until eventually the Commodore breaks through the interminable ceremony by saying, "Ah, so you are the notorious Lieutenant Pook, the human crab, without whom the Fleet cannot sail. Salaam, Pook Sahib."

Immediately the air is again thick with salaaming hands and arms, reminding me of picnickers attacked by bees.

"So, Pook Sahib, I trust you remembered to change trains at Tippee?" the Commodore inquires by way of small talk.

"No, sir, I stayed on the train while they altered the rails," I tell him bitterly, to forestall further Ramsami badinage.

However, everybody laughs, declaring me to be a typical British Sahib of the first water who jokes in the face of adversity. Simultaneously they point to their heads, but just as I am about to take them up on this rude gesture Honners informs me that they are admiring my golden coiffure.

"We are wishing to ascertain how you tuck such luxuriant curls inside your diving-helmet, Lieutenant Pook," the Commodore says.

"I force them in with my enormous hands," I reply, holding up those fists which, as you may recall, put Fireman Tucker away in the third round after he had made a similar remark during our memorable encounter at Southampton.

Fortunately we are diverted by distant shouts of, "Down with British Imperialism!" and "The English must go!" being chanted outside the station. Just as I begin to wonder if these are the local reaction to my arrival Commodore Gooji explains, "Ah, our impulsive students are on the march. What a grand sight to greet you as you enter Shaggapore for the first time, Lieutenant Pook."

"Quit Ramsam! Down with the British Parasite! Long live the Japanese!" echo the strident cries of the students. "Give us back our country! We demand Independence! Clear out, English Pig!"

"Come, let us watch our brave students demonstrating," the Commodore shouts excitedly, leading the way to the window in the R.T.O.'s office. "We shall be just in time to see them pouring by as they march on the British Embassy."

From the balcony it is an impressive sight to see such enthusiasm among the young as they stamp past with banners demanding the removal of the British Raj's heel from the neck of prostrate Ramsam. The students catch sight of the Commodore's flamboyant uniform and shout up at him, "Down with the British Tyrant! Up with the Japanese Liberator!"

"Hang the English Dogs!" the Commodore roars back at them.

"We want Independence!" the R.T.O. Officers chorus vigorously.

But shouting loudest of all is Honners at the rear. "Kick the British out! " he screams, throwing back his head to obtain more volume. "Away with Imperialism! Ramsam for the Ramsamis! Shoot the rotten Limeys! Hooray! . . ."

There is so much noise and shouting that nobody hears Honners hit the floor as I clout him with my business hand. Dazedly he tries to sit up as he wonders what has thumped him so effectively, but the sobering experience has completely taken his mind off his rabble-rousing activities.

"Who the hell done me?" he keeps repeating vaguely.

"I done you, mate - and you'll get done again if you start the Quit Ramsam war-chant once more. I can understand the locals getting worked up, but you and I are supposed to be English - with a war on our hands, don't forget. I haven't been here ten minutes and there's you screaming your head off for booting us out of the country. You must be off your rocker."

Honners picks himself up and groans miserably. "You've got it all wrong, Peter. The students march on the British Embassy whenever Foreign Aid is getting as low as the plughole, so everyone joins in for the hell of it. Actually they're terrified at the mere mention of Independence - they'd be bankrupt in a week - but the odd demonstration keeps the British Government on its toes and shakes up the coffers. If the students do the American Embassy next week you must come along - it's worth seeing. In fact we'll make up a party and join in. We all clench our fists and sing the *Red Flag* - that brings the dollars in as fast as sin. We never parade outside the Russian Embassy because they won't send any money - only leaflets and more diving gear."

I try to absorb the ramifications of international intrigue as best I can, so all I say is, "But the war, Honners - remember? What about the Jap Fleet steaming west across the Indian Ocean? What about the *Soonong* waiting for me so she can streak out through the Bay of Bengal like a speedboat on a mercy dash . . . ?"

"Ah, my honoured guest, now what do you think of our brave students?" rumbles the voice of Commodore Gooji who has at last torn himself away from the balcony. "What spirit, what patriotism beats within their youthful bosoms! Welcome to Shaggapore - the gayest city in all Ramsam. Tonight we are holding a Grand Mobilization Ball at the Imperial Shaggapore Gymkhana, Pook Sahib. Not often do we of the Orient have the human crab among us - therefore we make the most of you with a great feasting. All the Naval Staff will be there, so you shall meet Commander Bray and a hundred other lions of the deep. Then tomorrow we shall inspect the new diving-bell the Russians have so kindly given us for use on board the *Soonong,* and you can have a word with Commander Bray about the mighty bathysphere our Nawab is at present endeavouring to borrow from the French Government for your convenience."

"But I was under the impression it was all go, sir -boilers bursting and full steam ahead," I protest, deeming it wise at present not to delve further into the matter of diving-bells, bathysphere and conveniences.

"Ha, ha! All go! - delightful Western expression, Pook Sahib. All go it is indeed - all go to the Grand Mobilization Ball. Of course you would be at sea tonight but one cannot possibly sail during the Festival of Pijee, as you know."

The company hiss and hold up their hands at the prospect of a ship leaving port during the Festival of Pijee. Apparently such a vessel would founder like a brick.

"Then when do we sail?" I inquire hopelessly.

"Immediately after the Festival of Pijee of course, provided the ship has been blessed by the Gondahs. As sophisticated as you are, Pook Sahib, you of all people would not countenance embarking on a hazardous voyage of war in an unblessed ship during a time of religious celebration - that I will wager on,"

"Preposterous notion," Honners chimes in strongly. "Peter is not such a fool as he looks - he knows better than to flout the basic code of naval strategy."

What worries me now is that even to me it is beginning to sound like a preposterous notion I have been guilty of suggesting. In fact in my present fatigued state it appears impossible for the *Soonong* ever to sail again - always assuming that there was a time in the past when the overwhelming requirements of the Navy were satisfied to such an extent that she was permitted to leave the jetty.

"Meanwhile, Pook Sahib, you will be quartered at the Hotel Independence, because, as you are probably aware, no Europeans are permitted on board ship after sunset during the Festival of Pijee - for obvious reasons."

"No lights? What about Commander Bray then?"

"He also is staying at the Hotel Independence, together with all European officers of the Fleet. You will remain there until the Festival of Toolu commences, when naturally you will be enabled to live on the *Soonong.*"

"Who is Toolu, for pity's sake?"

"Toolu is Pijee's brother. It is during the Festival of Toolu that the Gondahs will bless your ship prior to sailing."

The whole complicated set-up is too much for me in my present state, and already my mind is subconsciously toying with the idea of asking for a posting to N.H.Q., so I cry "Enough", and let Honners put me in a horse-drawn tonga which waddles round to the Hotel Independence, my temporary quarters.

En route I notice with what pleasure is left to me that the sidewalks are liberally sprinkled with some of the most attractive girls I have ever seen. They hip along so upright that one automatically imagines them carrying pots on their heads of shimmering black hair, and they have the habit of suddenly raising their eyes to get you in their sights like marksmen at Bisley. I smile at every one who passes and in return they laugh gaily, acknowledging my attention with that delightful Ramsami gesture of holding the nose between thumb and index finger.

Fortunately I am almost immune from their wiles, having overcome the lusts of the body by means of violent physical exercise, beautiful thoughts, and an absorbing hobby. This latter occupation is photography, but it must be admitted that recently my album seems to contain nothing except pictures of girls. Furthermore, since coming to the East I have witnessed my violent physical exercises narrow to the field of dancing, and the beautiful thoughts have had to be abandoned completely since I read Freud.

Nevertheless I take careful stock of the female situation for future investigation in the realms of photography, but when I reflect that the ritual involved in meeting one of these lovelies must be so complex and lengthy as to be next to impossible I fall asleep in the tonga.

TWO

I lie on the cot in my hotel room too exhausted even for a single beautiful thought, so it is surprising that the noise from the next room eventually arouses me. By pressing my ear to the wall like a suction-cup I can make out some of the foulest language I have ever heard outside of England, so I assume the occupant is another frustrated Briton bemoaning the tardiness of the Ramsami war effort. To make matters more intriguing, not only are the hoarse oaths being delivered in a London accent which seems familiar but the speaker appears to be addressing himself.

Omitting the vile language, I hear the following: "Pijee, Pijee - all I hear is Pijee this, Pijee that. Turned off my own ship because of Pijee. Can't sail because of Pijee. Can't do damn-all because of Pijee. No Pook because of Pijee; and after Pijee comes his brother Toolu - Toolu, Brother of Darkness. Oh, my cursed luck . . ." and so on, over and over again.

To get some peace I bang on the wall with my chillum but this action seems to drive my neighbour berserk.

"Dare bang my wall! Come in here, you son of Pijee and I'll bang you straight back through the bulkhead, you . . ." and so on.

I don't take that kind of lip from any crackpot, let alone a stranger, so now I'm wide awake and ready to belt him through his own bulkhead if necessary. Springing off my cot I leave the room in a hurry and bowl straight in to his -livid.

I get a flash of a large naval officer sitting on a bunk, swigging magga, but at the sight of me he puts down the bottle and shouts, "Who the hell are you? Goldilocks or something?"

"And who the hell are you? Baldy or something?" I shout back. "If you want to use foul language just close your dead-lights first or I'll do it for you, mate - else you go straight through the deckhead."

I believe in the direct approach when dealing with riff-raff, and the man is so flabbergasted that he merely splutters with rage. Then he says, "You'll do what, Goldilocks?"

"Straight through the deckhead, hearing-aid and all, same as I did to Fireman Tucker of Southampton," I tell him in case he's deaf as well as thick. "No Pijee formalities - just *bop.*"

"Why, you impudent young punk, I'll break every bone in your body," he roars optimistically, jumping in and grabbing my throat with a remarkably large pair of hands. I prefer them at close quarters because it enables me to whip up my knee with practised skill before they are carried away for medical attention, but just as I am about to perform this manoeuvre there is a tap on the door and a beautiful girl enters carrying another bottle of magga.

Hurriedly we put each other down and face the girl. My attacker laughs and says to me, "Well, Goldilocks, that should give you the hang of it for the waltz tonight at the Mobilization Ball. The tango is much the same but more jerky. Just follow the band and you'll do fine."

"Thanks a million, Baldy - it should be a dance to remember, if you intend to fill the floor," I reply, taking my cue smoothly and slanting the last remark to include the fellow's lumbering bulk.

"Who is this young officer, Ginger? I know everyone in Shaggapore, but he's new," says the girl with understandable interest. This really has the big oaf in a quandary as he tries to think who his dancing-pupil is, so I keep quiet and survey the girl-friend. She is dark, with butterfly eyebrows and advertisement teeth, and wears that becoming Ramsami dress which is a cross between a saree and a kimono, called a dupa. She is quite tall and extremely well grouped. Her name is Rana. Already one of my beautiful thoughts enters my mind. but I hastily dismiss it with the resolution that I will have her in my album instead.

Ginger is still scratching the woolly hair which borders his bald pate as he tries to think of my name. He mutters, "I've seen the slob somewhere but can't just place him."

"Perhaps his name is Bubbles," Rana laughs, fingering the golden curls in wonder, "though I must say it seems odd finding you teaching someone to dance when you don't even know his name."

This tickles Ginger's fancy because he pulls Rana on to his knee and has her pour out three pegs of magga. "That's a damn good name - Bubbles! Yes, we'll stick at Bubbles. That suit you, Bubbles?"

"I've been called most things in my time, so why not Bubbles, eh, Baldy?" I agree cheerfully. But Baldy's new name offends his dignity and he lets me know it.

"Those aren't there just to prevent my shoulders getting sunburnt," he reminds me, pointing to the three gold bars on the epaulets of a shirt which hangs behind the door. Usually I don't miss much, so the shirt comes as a bit of a shock. I repress a forlorn hope that it might belong to Rana.

"Oh, really? Mine are to hide the size of my thumping muscles," I explain. "Not that they do it very well," I add, shrugging the shoulders which put paid to Bandsman Bangle at Chatham.

Baldy seems to be getting excited again. He says, "Exactly - they don't do it very well because there's only two of them. Two little gold bars don't even conceal the lowest form of life - such as you, for instance."

Instinctively I sense that the conversation is becoming personal and even as I am telling him that three bars are symbolic of the grating in a gutter I know I am in trouble. We both jump to our feet as though the National Anthem is being played, but Rana intervenes quickly. "Please sit down and stop quarrelling, boys. No one can possibly want to fight during the Festival of Pijee - it is a time of love and friendship in our country."

Gazing at Rana's lovely high cheekbones I can well believe this, and I could love her even out of Pijee season. However, she couldn't have made a more tactless remark to Baldy, whose bloodshot eyeballs dilate at the mention of the Festival. Gulping down another peg of magga he announces, "I've sailed the sea from the Arctic Ocean to the Magellan Straits but never have I been pushed around by such a crazy bunch as this godforsaken Shaggapore lot. I've been here nigh on two months trying to get out of harbour in command of what they humorously call a man-o-war. Two months of frustration enough to drive a matelot up the stack...."

"Have another magga, darling," Rana suggests, glad that Pijee has taken his mind off me. He drinks it without looking at it.

"The only conclusion you can draw is that we're intended to put to sea on a pilgrimage, not a voyage. To make matters worse, my chief diver hasn't turned up to take charge of enough salvage equipment to raise the entire Japanese Fleet. Then comes the last straw - not allowed to stay on my own ship after sunset! The priests usher me off because I'm unclean, if you've ever heard of such twaddle in this day and age."

"What's her name then?" I butt in, intrigued by the mention of a Diving Officer.

"Rana," he replies distractedly.

"No, I mean your ship."

"Oh, the *Soonong*. But do you know what really broke my spirit? The merciless shower sent me up to N.H.Q. at Jawanagar twice, just to get me out of the way. *Twice,* mark you."

"Did you remember to change at Tippee?" I inquire.

Only Rana's prompt intervention prevents him from becoming actively hostile, so I decide to conceal my identity at this particular moment and turn the conversation to Rana.

"You're the most beautiful girl I've ever seen," I announce simply, believing in the direct approach plus high-pressure.

"Oh, thank you, Bubbles," she croons, swirling her long black hair with pleasure. "Unless you're only saying that because it's true."

"Yes, I agree," Baldy leers at me, "that's why I've been going out with her for the past month."

"So who will you be going out with next month?" I ask him, taking Rana's hand to feel if her honey-brown skin can really be as smooth as it looks. Baldy's eyes slit possessively and he emits a kind of primeval mating challenge, so Rana oils him up with a solution.

"You two boys mustn't fight over me," she smiles, giving me eyes like automobile-flashers. "We must show our hospitality to Bubbles by introducing him to some of the local girls."

"We sure must," Baldy agrees emphatically, putting a leg-o-mutton arm round Rana's bare shoulders, "we don't want Bubbles becoming part of the old eternal triangle - the flat bit at the base."

Before I can correct his faulty geometry there is a knock at the door, to which Rana responds. Outside stands a Ramsami naval officer in full dress who proves to be an outrider preparing the way for the entrance of Commodore Gooji.

"Show the Commodore in," Baldy says disinterestedly. "It's time we had the daily bulletin of confusion, mystery, and delay.

Tell him if any more diving equipment has arrived the ship'll keel over."

At the Commodore's entrance we all stand up, salaam, and drone the traditional greetings about taking salt and inquiring after our ancestors and invoking a population-explosion on our wives in the shape of seven sons. "Ah, so in your businesslike British way you have forestalled me, Lieutenant Pook," he observes, staring past me to the magga bottle. "It seems that already you have introduced yourself to Commander Bray."

Mention of my name has a deleterious effect on the latter in that he is struck dumb, so I bridge the gap by extending to Commodore Gooji the hospitality of the magga tray. Whereupon he throws up his beringed hands in dismay.

"Ah, Lieutenant Pook, you have not yet learned that we Ramsamis are forbidden to let strong waters touch our lips at any time - least of all during the Festival of Pijee."

The appearance of the Commodore's nose tempts me to ask if the Ramsamis have mastered the art of drinking without using their lips.

"What is more important, Lieutenant Pook, here at Shaggapore we are concentrating all our efforts, mustering all our forces, and girding all our loins for the immediate and relentless pursuit of the Nippon Enemy. Every pleasure is being set aside, every personal preoccupation is being relegated to the background, that the Foe may be stalked by land and sea as a prelude to his urgent and utter destruction. No pebble is being left unturned; no avenue is not being explored, the better to . . . ."

"Here we go again," Commander Bray mutters bitterly, pouring out four burra pegs of magga.

"Here at Shaggapore under your very eyes our Fleet is being prepared and tuned to concert pitch, that it may leap out from the Bay of Bengal to seize the unsuspecting foe by the throat and send him hurtling down the abyss of defeat like a shark tearing the heart out of a whale - flinging the   ...."

"Don't forget the Nawab of Ramsam," Commander Bray reminds the Commodore, yawning his head off.

"Ah, indeed - well spoken. What an example we have in our gallant Nawab of Ramsam, the Vulture of the Orient -

'Collecting all his might, dilated stood,
Like Teneriff or Atlas, unremoved:
His stature reached the sky, and on his crest
Sat Horror plumed; nor wanted in his grasp
What seemed both spear and shield.'

- directing our work, instigating our plans, guiding our strategy, exhorting our people, pooling our resources, and leading us to final victory. Gentlemen, let us remember our mighty Raj of the North ...."

Transported by his own oratory the Commodore allows his zeal for remembering the Nawab to make him forget his condition of temperance, to the extent that he sweeps up a glass with a passionate cry of "Long live our gallant Nawab." Then, as we all follow suit, he gulps down the liquor in a fever of patriotism and thirst.

"Thank you, gentlemen," the Commodore booms as we implore Providence to grant the Nawab an extension of years beyond his life expectancy. "Now let us couple another illustrious name with our Nawab - the Pardishah of your Island Home, the King of England."

Glasses are charged for the toast, which is followed by "The gallant *Soonong* and all who sail in her, if ever," proposed with a trace of cynicism by Commander Bray. Not to be outdone, I give them "The Commodore and all who serve at N.H.Q."

By the time we have honoured Ramsami Railways and the

Shaggapore Gas, Light, & Coke Undertaking, Rana has to visit the bar for more magga in order that we may not overlook personal toasts such as Commander Bray, myself, and the more spectacular charms of Rana. Then the Commodore prepares to leave with some difficulty, but his native dignity never forsakes him. Even at the door he manages to turn for his farewell speech.

"Ah, Lieutenant Pook, happy I am to know that you have seen and experienced in this very room the matchless spirit of camaraderie which exists in our ancient Navy, whereby each man sacrifices personal gain for the common weal. Let me put it to you - what chance has the enemy against such loyalty? What chance has the foe in the face of such hearts of oak? What chance has the invader against such intrepid comrades."

"What chance have we of sailing against them then, sir?" I exclaim, carried away by his eloquence and impatient to be in the thick of battle.

Commodore Gooji gives me a distasteful glare and calls out from the hall, "I shall expect you gentlemen to join me later tonight at 2200 hours in the Alabaster Bar of the Imperial Ballroom. Till then, salaam Sahibs, salaam Memsahib."

THREE

The very magnitude of the Imperial Ballroom really leaves me breathless. Although you could put Hammersmith Palais quite comfortably in the Alabaster Bar alone, it is the colours which make me gape and probably explain why so many of the Ramsamis are wearing dark glasses. Against the static colours of the colonnades flit the flashing dupas and sarees of the ladies and the white and gold uniforms of the officers over a glass floor of multi-coloured panels lighted from below.

Music is supplied by two bands; one the local Ramsami Railway dance-band of some thirty players, the other the Ramsami State Orchestra of sixty-eight musicians. As they are at opposite ends of the ballroom they are both playing simultaneously without causing discord, but for the dancers it is disconcerting at the half-way mark - where they have to decide whether to continue tangoing or stand to attention for the National Anthem.

The latter is for the entry of the Nawab of Ramsam and his delightful Nawabani. Also in their retinue are the Lieutenant Governor, Chiefs of Staff, Commodore Gooji, Officials of State, and me. I am in the party by accident. Originally I was drinking magga with Commander Bray in the Alabaster Bar for Europeans Only, as it is called in this dry country, under the toastmastership of Commodore Gooji. Half-way through the toast to Allied Navies, Confusion to our Enemies, and a Speedy Victory, the Commodore suddenly mutters something in Ramsami and exits left in a hurry. Thinking he is going to the Gents, and having already failed to find it myself among the dizzy porticos and enormous antechambers, I follow him at the double.

We gallop past several uniformed chuprassis who have previously answered my inquiries as to the location of the Gents by guiding me back to my friends at the bar, with the explanation that "Here are your Gents, Sahib, standing by the counter just as you left them."

Eventually two tall Sikh soldiers espy Commodore Gooji's portly figure approaching and they open the biggest pair of toilet doors I have ever seen - thirty feet high and twelve feet broad. Following eagerly on the Commodore's heels I unexpectedly find myself up front on the dais of the Presence Chamber and towering over the Nawab and his petite Nawabani. Facing me, but lower down on the floor of the ballroom, is the surprised countenance of Commander Bray who is standing rigidly to attention in the front rank of the 2,000 guests.

Although the Nawab keeps scowling sideways at me, there is nothing I can do unless I leap down from the dais or pretend to faint. Apparently everyone decides to carry on as though all is normal, because the band strikes up the National Anthem which is followed, incongruously enough, by "I do like to be beside the Seaside."

At the conclusion of this musical medley everybody on the dais walks slowly backwards, bowing and salaaming to the Nawab.

Being unaccustomed to this mode of regression I reverse until something hard touches the back of my thighs, causing me to sit down suddenly. Obviously my etiquette is causing some concern among the assembly because Commodore Gooji hastily leans over my shoulder to whisper something about getting off the

Imperial Throne this instant for Pijee's sake you useless dung-carrier.

Although this expression is local idiom for what is practically a term of endearment, the way he mouths it gives me dangerous red flashes before my eyes, causing me to debate momentarily the fate of lieutenants who flatten Commodores on Presence Chamber floors. However, my mind is taken off such speculations by the Nawab himself. He glides over the carpet in his tight shantung jeans and knee-length floral robe, smiles graciously, and says, "We have heard of your exploits, Lieutenant Pook, but as yet to the best of our knowledge you have not taken over our Imperial Throne."

Highly embarrassed I get off his marble billet so he can occupy his rightful position, apologize profusely, and shuffle backwards. However, the Nawabani detains me with the question, "Ah, Lieutenant Pook, the ladies of the Purdah are curious to discover how you cause your hair to protrude so golden and curly even with your naval cap on. To us this is a most unusual spectacle, evoking much interest among us."

Making a slow low kowtow bow to the lady I reply truthfully, "I don't do anything myself, ma'am - it just sprouts up like that from the roots, and I'd look silly wearing a hair-net."

"Thank you, Lieutenant Pook," she replies charmingly. "Now you have answered my question so frankly I would like to answer one of yours. What do you wish to know about our country?"

Repressing a question as to the location of the Gents I say boldly, "When does the Fleet sail, ma'am?"

"Ah, that is outside a woman's province, young man. Who is knowing the great secrets of State? Please ask me something within my power to enlighten you."

"Ma'am, will you do me the honour of having the first dance with me?" Frankly I am not madly keen to dance with anyone at the moment but I figure this would get me off the dais with dignity and let Commodore Gooji see I am in royal favour.

The Nawabani glances at the Nawab who waves a bejewelled hand towards the floor and sniffs loudly, to indicate either that he prefers to sit this one out or that he wants me off the dais without delay. This seems to be the signal for general dancing because the glass floor crowds rapidly, filling the great ballroom with the rustle of dupas and the chink of medals. Nobody speaks. Instead they circle around us, bowing to the Nawabani who returns the compliments with regal dignity. I also return them to be on the safe side in the matter of Court etiquette.

The aged Lieutenant-Governor can hardly bow at all, what with his uniform, medals, sash, cummerbund, and other luggage of office and tradition. His sword trails the floor like a hockey stick, setting up no mean hazard for the other dancers.

As we navigate our way through the Ramsami aristocracy the Nawabani suddenly looks up at me to say, "Tell me, Lieutenant Pook, is it true what we are hearing - that you are known far and wide as the human crab?

"I'm sorry, ma'am, but what with all these people milling around us, and you having to acknowledge their bows, I can't help dancing awkwardly," I explain. To make matters worse, my left hand completely envelops her own tiny mitt as though she is wearing a boxing-glove.

"No, no, dear boy - I was not referring to your lack of skill on the dance-floor but to your prowess under water," she laughs. "I ask because my husband is extremely interested in deep-sea diving, believing that the diver is the eyes and ears of the Fleet."

"Has he been down himself, ma'am?" I inquire cautiously.

When I am in about twenty fathoms I sometimes don't know which way is up, or even where I am, let alone serve as the eyes and ears of the Fleet. During my first real dive I recall wondering whether my helmet was on back-to-front or they had lowered me into liquid mud.

The Nawabani gives me a flashing smile, saying with a gesture of fantasy, "Oh, no, Lieutenant Pook, my husband is not a great lover of the ocean. To be exact, he has never been on it, let alone under it. Nevertheless it intrigues him immensely, and of late we have been favoured by another large shipment of diving equipment from America worth over a lakh of rupees. Thus we are the proud owners of more equipment than is possessed by any State this side of Calcutta. Can you descend to a depth in excess of twenty metres?"

"Oh, shallow stuff, ma'am. We call that mere paddling - just enough to get your boots wet," I throw off airily. However I make a mental note to check on metres at the first opportunity, in case they are longer than feet. But the Nawabani stops dancing in mid-chassé and declares, "Here *he* is," with a note of awe in her voice. Assuming it is an Excuse Me dance, I step politely aside in deference to the aged Lieutenant-Governor himself, but instead of saying "Robbers", as is customary in this particular manoeuvre, he indicates that he wishes to be introduced. I note that he is decked out in the regalia of a bygone age until he resembles the great Duke of Wellington the week he died. His Aide-de-Camp, who accompanies him everywhere including the dance-floor, does the honours.

"His Excellency the Lieutenant-Governor Surgeon Rear-Admiral Sir Bertram Donnington-Buckett, Bart., G.C.S.I., G.B.E., G.C.I.E., K.C.I.E., K.C.V.O., . . . " he rambles on as though reading off an eye-chart.

"Lieutenant Pook," I reply, bowing suitably low.

The venerable Lieutenant-Governor is very pleased to meet me, but he is putting on his bifocals to inspect my medal-ribbons like a dealer at a stamp auction. Judging from his own display, one thing is certain - I can't have any gongs up which he hasn't got.

"Ho, ho, young fellow, not often we see the Boxer Rebellion of '99 these days, eh?" he chuckles, bending forward to support himself on my chest. "To think that Queen Victoria handed that to you personally, my word. You don't look a day over sixty either. What memories you must treasure, my boy."

As he is now working along the row to my American Army Star for sleeping out-of-doors, I hastily change the subject by asking him when he thinks the Fleet will sail. Even as the words leave my lips I know it is a mistake.

"Ho, ho, young fellow, you're new here and full of the old bulldog spirit, eh? Impatient to 'Pluck bright honour from the pale-fac'd moon, Or dive into the bottom of the deep, Where fathom-line could never touch the ground, And pluck up drownéd honour by the locks,' eh, me lad? You must learn that in the Orient we don't bandy great secrets of State about in public, what? Nor do we wish to unleash the dogs of war during a festivity such as this. But mark my words, young fellow-me-lad, when we do - when we do, I say - gad, then we shall see the proud foe crushed underfoot by our hearts of oak. . . .

> 'All furnish'd, all in arms,
> All plum'd like estridges that wing the wind,
> Baited like eagles having lately bath'd,
> Glittering in golden coats, like images,
> As full of spirit as the month of May,
> And gorgeous as the sun at midsummer,
>
> Wanton as youthful goats, wild as young bulls.
> I saw young Harry, with his beaver on,
> His coshes on his thighs, gallantly arm'd,
> Rise from the ground like feather'd Mercury,

And vaulted with such ease into his seat,
As if an angel dropp'd down from the clouds,
To turn and wind a fiery Pegasus
And witch the world with noble horsemanship'."

    I speculate if any horse will be able to support me in my diving-bell but say nothing because the speech has inspired everybody as much as it has exhausted the LieutenantGovernor, who is being assisted to a chair and brandy by his Aide. Now it is clear to me that even the Russian agents must despair of getting the sailing date out of this lot, so I decide to mark time and enjoy myself instead.

    "Isn't it about time you tore yourself away from the royal circle and mixed with the rabble?" inquires an irate voice behind me. It is Commander Bray escorting a radiant Rana. "A fine dance you've led me so far tonight, Pook -gate-crashing the Imperial clique like that. What have you got to say for yourself?"

    "Where's the Gents?"

    "Have you no soul, man? Here you are, playing Anna and the King of Siam at the Imperial Shaggapore Gymkhana, yet all that's on your tiny mind are the basic functions of life. Where's your finer feelings? Where's your sense of destiny? Anyway, if you must know, see that half-mile corridor behind the band? Well, it's along there, right at the end. They ought to lay on a rickshaw service to it. Then come back here and have a drink with the working classes."

    Some time later I return to my party as requested. We are sitting at a table about due west from the band, watching a half-caste girl sing "You Are My Sunshine." Although the magga is flowing pretty freely I can't help noticing that every time she comes to the "You are my sunshine" bit she looks across at me. It is so obvious that eventually Commander Bray leans over to ask me, "What's your name then?"

"Sunshine, I guess, judging by the lass with the delicate stare."

"Must be his yellow hair," Commander Bray remarks to himself.

I look encouragingly at the singer and giggle naively every time she comes to my new name in case she thinks I am thick, but I am hardly prepared for the next move. Finishing the song, she descends from the dais, hips slowly across to our table, extends a bangle-laden arm and says, "Come, Sunshine, let us dance."

Although a cosmopolitan type I am not just a woman's plaything, so I act hard-to-get by throwing away some crisp party badinage to prove I am not stunned by the invitation. Nevertheless, I am on the floor and holding her before she can change her mind, but she seems to like it. She looks up at me with the biggest brown eyes I have ever seen, and says, "My, my, Sunshine - you must be all of two metres tall."

"No, dear, I'm barely six-feet-three-stunted, you might say," I reply modestly, having just checked with Commander Bray about metres. One advantage of height is that, having lowered my right hand in successive stages down the girl's back without contacting fabric, I seem to be clasping a nude woman in public. However, by holding her away from me momentarily, I see that she is wearing a red ball-gown lower down, so all is well.

For a while there is no conversation as we find the best position for dancing romantically through the war-torn cream of Ramsami society. If small talk is needed there is always Pijee or changing at Tippee to fall back on, but the girl eventually whispers in my ear, "So you are knowing well the Nawab, the Lieutenant-Governor, and Commodore Gooji, eh? All the big nobs, in fact."

I confess to some intimacy with the top brass, but mention nothing about the Gents episode of course. Instead I inquire as to her name. It is Tina, so in exchange she calls me Peter. Dancing close to Tina takes my mind clean off the war, and for the first time since coming to Ramsam I don't care whether the Fleet sails or sinks. Furthermore, lotus perfume of such density wells up from her warm body that I am compelled to catch my breath as though I have pleurisy of the lungs.

To be frank there is only one snag about Tina. Like everyone else around here, she seems to have diving on the brain. This is a queer set-up because before long we are alone together out on the marble patio beneath the stars, clasped tenderly in each other's arms and whispering lovers' secrets about air-pressure and outlet-valves. A passer-by might think I am murmuring Donne's lyrics to my beloved, whereas in actual fact I am satisfying this beautiful girl's morbid desire to hear the Recompression Tables from my own lips.

I know it is ridiculous but I just can't get her off the subject. However, being a practical man, well used to the idiosyncrasies of women and how to jolly them along, I play it up. After all, once in South America I courted an heiress whose idea of the perfect evening was to tell me about metallurgy by the hour, which taught me the art of making love even during the trying conditions of learning to extract gold-bearing ore from the very bowels of the earth some 3,000 feet below where we were sitting in her flat.

Sensing a long session in front of me, I bring in the history of diving as from the time of the Ancient Greeks, but when I reach the exciting part concerning one Corporal Harris working on the wreck of the *Royal George* at Spithead in 1839 wearing the first diving-dress as we know it today, Tina reluctantly tears herself from my arms to sing her finale.

I return to Commander Bray and Rana, who don't seem all that thrilled to see me. He says, "Well, you certainly fall on your feet every time, Peter. A complete stranger, yet you pick up the loveliest girl in the place... except you, dear, of course," he adds hastily to Rana. "Who is she, anyway?"

Rana scowls and shrugs her brown shoulders. "I am not knowing this singing girl. She is not one of our set at all. Probably imported by the band."

Commander Bray gazes across to Tina who is up on the dais putting over a number with that pseudo-American accent most unlike her normal voice. "You don't waste time, Peter, that's for sure," he grins at me. "How do you find her?"

"Well, she's wonderful - a sort of movie job come true, but so far her interest seems centred on my diving experiences. Her idea of married bliss may well be life for two inside a diving-bell."

Commander Bray's attitude tenses with surprising rapidity. "You mean she's been pumping you about salvage operations?"

"Certainly has. So I gave her the run-around from the popular Press - nothing secret or anything like that. You know the kind of dross; slipping the weights, blowing up, the bends, urination under pressure, how to clear your ears - the usual chitchat between lovers."

"Could be she's a spy like Rana - the place seems full of them."

"May well be - she asked me when the Fleet sails."

"Did you tell her?"

"Could the Nawab himself? I'm not psychic."

"Exactly, Peter. That's partly why I keep in with Rana. She won't let on who she's in with, but at least she keeps me posted about the Navy. Otherwise I'd know precious little, believe me. All I need now is to get a friend who's in the priesthood - that's the Gondah wallahs - and then I'll have my very own little built-in spy ring. Won't that be cosy for a man who's captain of his own ship?"

This startling development takes me some time to digest because the girls usually fall for me for what I am, not what I know. In fact one once told me in Shanghai that she was attracted to me because I didn't seem to know anything. I ask Commander Bray, "What's the form then if Tina really is a spy?"

He draws on his cigarette and looks at me sideways. "What does it matter so long as she's nice to you, Peter? There's nothing you can tell her from the Service angle except how much they pay you, but she can probably keep you in the picture. Let me know how it goes and pass on any buzzes you can pick up from her - little points such as when I'm to be allowed back on my own ship. Meanwhile keep her happy with the story of your life under water. Why worry? - the money's good, so enjoy yourself in the mysterious East while you can.... Watch it, Peter, here she comes again. Better stick with Rana and me for a bit while we double-check."

Tina high-heels it over to our table to sit very close to me, but she doesn't mention anything about matters sub-aqua. Rana eyes her distastefully, leaving Commander Bray and myself to stoke up the party - which we do in true naval fashion. Tina soon reveals herself to be a personality in her own right, declaring that Commander Bray is her ideal of the British sea-dog come to life, and if it were not for my presence she could let herself be swept into his big strong arms. This approach appeals to the Commander, who responds with appropriate sea-dog anecdotes of his adventures in South America, Japan, Australia, and the China Coast. It is noticeable that the denouement of each story turns on the women he has attracted and the fate of jealous rivals who foolishly crossed his path.

Seizing upon a lead while he refills the glasses, I recount the absorbing description of what I did to Fireman Tucker of Southampton in the third round under similar circumstances. Whereupon Commander Bray playfully chucks me under the chin to demonstrate where Fireman Tucker's tactics were at fault. It seems I can learn the lesson more clearly by listening to Commander Bray's epic encounter with Able Seaman Couch at Nagasaki in '36, a bout without parallel in the annals of the ring wherein the Commander, overcoming every disadvantage of height, weight, reach, and Service prejudice, bedevilled with malaria, handicapped by a broken knuckle, dissipated by drink and women, hopelessly behind on points, manages to fell the giant Seaman after 2 minutes 49 seconds of the last round.

I yawn widely as the Commander tells us how his opponent is counted out and victory announced simultaneously with the final bell. The two girls understandably fail to see the point of the climax, but the moral has not been lost on me. Observing how Tina wishes the Commander would keep the conversation in a more romantic channel, I exercise my customary tact by taking her on the floor for another dance, where we discover that life away from the Commander's table has a lot to recommend it.

"He's gauche, but means well, dear," I explain, to let her see I disapprove of braggarts. "He thinks he's the chief bull of the herd or something. At his age he should have learned that you don't make love like you're a wounded gorilla at bay."

Tina winds her arm round my neck and kisses my jugular vein. "That I would like very much," she whispers esoterically.

About 4 a.m. when the ball is over, Tina and I jog home happily in a tonga for two, enjoying the cooler air of the night which we find refreshing in the extreme. I have already dated her for the following evening, so I am set for a steady romance with Eastern trimmings. She possesses that abundance of beauty perfectly coordinated with feminine charm which make Ramsami women so attractive to Englishmen.

Consequently I feel downright naive when I hear myself asking her the ludicrous question, "Tell me straight, darling, are you anything to do with the espionage game - or to put it bluntly, are you a spy?"

Tina's light laugh floats through the night at such a suggestion. "Ah, you delightful big Englishman, how utterly sweet of you - a spy! Lovely! What fantastic notions your Western films and novels put into your head! Mind, I'm not saying it doesn't sound fascinating or that it doesn't appeal to my sense of the dramatic - but really, Peter, can you imagine *me* as a spy?"

With her head archly on one side, her huge eyes upturned, and her lips parted she looks anything but at the moment, causing me to wish I had not asked such a lame question.

"Well, Tina, you were probing a bit deep about diving, out there on the patio."

At this she flings her arms around me to kiss delightedly.

"Oh, so that's the trouble, darling - oh, wonderful! Why, all the books on courtship and suchlike insist on the girl finding out all about her man's interests and then talking to him about them to flatter his ego. So, if you had been a numismatist I should have rambled on about old coins, and so on. In your case, your reputation as the human crab preceded your arrival, so naturally I was well primed beforehand, apart from the fact that here the common talk in the bazaars is of the *Soonong* and her extensive salvage equipment. But *me* a spy - oh, lovely! How my mother will be laughing when she is hearing this rare titbit!"

"I must be crazy," I admit, recalling bitterly that it was Commander Bray who put the idea in my head in the first place, and one can only wonder how far jealousy will drive a man to destroy his friend and fellow-officer. I have a long memory when it comes to revenge but this time I tie a mental knot in it for good measure. However, Tina seems to make light of the matter.

"Pooh, just forget the whole thing, Peter. Anyway we are near my apartment so we must leave each other till this evening. It's far too late to ask you in now."

The tonga pulls up outside a large white Colonial-type building in the northern outskirts of Shaggapore. It is so well lighted that our good-night kiss is performed under floodlights in full view of two armed sentries, whose duty, presumably, is to prevent Tina's admirers storming the place in a paroxysm of passion.

As I help Tina down from the rear of the tonga she whispers, "Night-night, honey; thanks for an unforgettable evening. Don't bother to come all the way down the drive. See you soon."

For some moments I stand there bemused by the glamour of my new girl-friend and the warm atmosphere of the tropical night. Contemplatively I take out a cigarette and stroll down the drive to catch a last glimpse of Tina before she disappears through the great wrought-iron gates of her home. By the look of things I have clicked with a girl in the money, and this sober thought does not make me melancholy.

Turning back towards the waiting tonga, I absent-mindedly scan the brass plate flanking the portico of the entrance. I read it several times in quick succession because the words strike a chord in my memory. It says: *Russian Embassy. Strictly No Admittance.*

FOUR

What with the deadlock of the Pijee Festival and the arrival of the Shilla, the notorious hot season, it seems that the rush to prepare the *Soonong* has been slowed down from Top Priority to that typical Ramsami pace which the European examines without being able to detect any form of movement. So, in company with Commander Bray, Honners, Rana, Tina, and everybody of note in Shaggapore, I spend a whole week lazing on the lawns by the swimming-pool of the Imperial Gymkhana.

The marble pool is shaped like a four-leaf clover and contains water so blue that when I dive into it I always feel it will dye my skin. Behind us is the veranda of the Europeans Only Pool Bar, whence chupprasis in white uniforms and red sashes glide out with drink-laden trays for the refreshment of the guests.

Commander Bray passes the time in reminiscence of bygone days round the China Coast, while Honners pores over textbooks in his endless struggle with the intricacies of the Ramsami language. Tina and Rana play an interminable succession of American records until I know every intonation and phrasing of the Crosby genius. In fact, when I die they may well find the words of "Pennies From Heaven" engraved on my heart.

As for myself, the humid heat and exotic surroundings are rapidly lulling me into a kind of torpor wherein I begin to wonder if the war is not some fiction which is preying on my mind following a visit to the cinema. My hints to Commander Bray that so far not only have I been nowhere near the *Soonong* but also I haven't even seen the ocean are countered by sleepy grunts to the effect that the heat down the docks is unbearable at the moment and that "During Pijee they won't let us on board anyway."

During an afternoon siesta I steal away from my party and take the elevator to the flat roof of the Gymkhana in order to do a little reconnaissance of my own. Stepping carefully over the slumbering bodies of Commodore Gooji and his Aides who are in conference in the flower-garden up here, I gain the parapet of the roof to peer southwards for my first glimpse of the sea.

Slowly my eyes become accustomed to the heat-haze which makes it difficult to distinguish where the earth meets the sky, but nowhere can I identify anything on which a ship could float. Behind me lie the low curve of the Shaggapore Ghats and the mullah through which the railway-line follows the River Umji down from Tippee. To the south is a flat plain on which every kind of tropical produce from plantains to rice is being cultivated, stretching out in all directions except northwards as far as the eye can see.

For some time the beauty and novelty of the panorama hold my attention so intently that the lack of ocean is forgotten, but after a while a vague picture enters my mind of the Fleet lying landlocked in some enormous pineapple orchard. In fact, up here in this dreamy tower overlooking the land of make-believe I wonder momentarily if the whole set-up of the Royal Ramsami Navy is perhaps an hallucination I am having as an inmate of some Oriental asylum.

Tearing myself away from the landscape I hurry below to my companions in search of information and crumbs of reassurance. All are slumbering in the shade of coloured umbrellas set out under picturesque litchi trees, so, throwing myself down beside Honners, I shake him gently from his siesta.

"Where's the sea? - where's the blessed ocean?" I demand excitedly of this prostrate warrior.

"All round the ship, you fool," he mumbles sleepily. "Where d'you think it is - down the funnel?"

"No, no, Honners, you're not at sea now - and never will be as far as I can make out. Where's the real sea - the floating stuff? Where's the docks and the Fleet?"

Without opening his slumber-riddled eyes, Honners makes a vague pointing gesture towards the Southern Cross. "Over there, mate - all wet and wavy."

"Then why can't I see it, that's what I want to know? How is it that the sea has coconut-palms, paddy fields, and grazing land all over it?"

This really has Honners sitting up wide awake. "You in for malaria or something, Peter?" he says worriedly. "What the devil are you raving about? Maybe you should wear a topee and spine-pad like they did in the old days."

"Look, Honners, I've been here a whole week or more without spotting so much as a bit of seaweed, let alone a warship. Put your cards on the table and tell me the worst. What is this Navy - a mirage? Aren't you tired of playing sailors like a load of kids?"

Honners looks hurt. "Really, Peter, since you arrived a fellow can't even have his afternoon zizz in peace. Of course it's a real Navy - else how would you and I be in it?"

"Then why can't I see so much as the top of a mast, that's what I want to know? You told me yourself that *Shaggapore* means where the ocean kisses the land. Well, where in hell does it do it? Or do they simply wheel the Fleet about on trolleys?"

"Oh, I see what you mean, Peter. I thought you knew that Shaggapore was once the greatest blunder next to Rangoon and Calcutta, but as the River Umji silted up so the sea got further and further away. Nowadays the blunder is well south down at Port

Chattoo because the Fleet can't navigate the Umji up to Shaggapore any further north than Chukkoo. You might say that the ocean kisses the land at Chattoo today, to be strictly accurate - not Shaggapore."

"Then why the devil aren't we all down at Chattoo or whatever you call the godforsaken hole?"

"For the simple reason that there aren't any hotels in a dump like Chattoo - they're all here at Shaggapore. Even Chuckoo is better than Chattoo."

"Then how, if the occasion should ever arise, do we get to Chattoo? Walk?"

"Heavens no - in this heat? We just get a gharry as far as Chuckoo, then go aboard a pulwah on to Chattoo. You can't take a pulwah from Shaggapore because the Umji is only navigable from Chukkoo."

By now I am too tired to sort it out, so all I do is ask resignedly, "Is it far?"

"Oh, no, Peter, not far by our standards, but by the time the gharry reaches Chukkoo you're dead beat and dehydrated. Then you have to change over to the pulwah and hope for a fair wind down to Chattoo - that takes time, of course."

"Roughly how long would you say - in years?"

"Well, Peter, it depends on the wind chiefly. Given the luck of the draw I've done it in two days. On the other hand when Commander Bray first went down he hit the Peyana - that's the seasonal sou'easter which rushes up the Umji -and was delayed at Chuckoo the best part of a week. Eventually he had them tow the pulwah by means of ropes and bullocks along the banks. By the way, Peter, never mention the Peyana to him, even in fun - he may become unhinged and do you a mischief."

"I know just how he feels, Honners - but why no motor transport? I realize it makes a terrible noise, but do you know the real reason? No cars, no planes - is it forbidden by Pijee or something? If the Nawab heard a Rolls Royce purring in the distance would it shatter his ear-drums and send him deaf?"

"Oddly enough, Peter, you're right for once. Mechanical transport does not find favour in the eyes of Pijee, but for my money the real reason is more practical. The Nawab is a shrewd old wallah who has seen what airlines and the like have done for other countries as small as Ramsam, bringing material progress but driving out the soul. Most important of all, in order to keep a stable monarchy the Nawab must maintain full employment, and nothing soaks up the spare bods like a railway. In fact, practically everyone here who isn't in the Navy works on the railway. To me it's as simple as that."

I gaze at young Honners for some time, thinking to myself here is a sharp boy who doesn't miss much. I wonder if he knows more, so I continue to pump him casually.

"How come the Fleet seems to be armed to the teeth with diving equipment, Honners? Have you fathomed that one?"

"Much more difficult," he confesses. "For Pijee's sake keep it under your topee, but I believe Bray has secret orders to search the Bay of Bengal for lost anchors - when he isn't actually engaged with the enemy. They say he's been given an Admiralty chart with the location of a dozen or more anchors marked on it."

"Sounds strange, but who are *they* who know all this?"

"Well, Peter, to be frank it isn't a they but a she. To be more precise, my girl-friend Shrini - so you can take it for what it's worth. Though she's usually pretty well on the ball, being in the espionage game for one of the big Powers."

By now I am so accustomed to spies that I refrain from comment.

"Why? - are we short of anchors, Honners?"

"Not so far as one can see, but apparently anchors are big stuff in the Pijee ritual, symbolizing the link between Pijee on one hand

and Mother Earth on the other. Recovering the anchors is an important prestige thing for the Nawab because not only does it enhance his reputation in the eyes of the people, but also it ensures his place in Tiboona."

"Where's that then? Another landlocked harbour?"

"Oh, Tiboona is the place where all good Ramsamis go when they die - up there," Honners explains, pointing northwards in the direction of the Himalayas. "It's a kind of celestial holiday-camp with mountains, run by Pijee and Toolu."

"I thought it was called N.H.Q."

Honners giggles. "No point in fighting it, Peter - the outlook and tempo here are completely different to the efficiency, pace and chaos of Belter Barracks back home. You want to lie back and enjoy it like I do, then you'll start appreciating life as much as the Ramsamis. They think we're mad, itching to rush off to battle and get ourselves axed-and they could well be right too."

"But you know how I detest hanging about trying to kill time. I like action - or at least some kind of routine."

"Then you'll soon get it, Peter. Pijee is nearly over, so then it's the green light in earnest with the Festival of Toolu. Once the ship is blest by the Gondahs, off we go -*zoom*- all spray and bow-wave. Personally, I don't beef overmuch because we're on a good thing and I intend staying on in this mob after the war, Pijee willing. It's Nature's answer to work."

On our left Commander Bray stirs sleepily in soporific pose. "Pipe down during siesta, Pook - that's an order," he grunts liverishly.

Apart from the heat, the journey down to Chattoo, via Chukkoo, strikes me as being quite a pleasant experience, once I have grown accustomed to the sight of a long line of horse-drawn gharries jogging along the road with their cargo of naval officers and retinue. Tina, Rana and Shrini accompany us as far as Chukkoo, as do numerous wives, children, and servants. Commodore Gooji's delightful laughing offspring fill two gharries, giving the expedition such an air of holiday picnic that we are loath to leave them behind at Chukkoo.

One of his daughters, Kulima, in particular often stares at my hair in wonderment, but when I turn to give the girl my attention she buries her face in her hands and giggles hysterically. Nothing is calculated to send one's dignity to pot more effectively. But here we must make sad farewell to the wives and sweethearts before boarding the light sailing pulwah for the last lap of the journey to Chattoo.

"Well, Peter, let's hope you're satisfied now," Honners says to me when he can no longer see Shrini's figure back on the jetty. "That's good-bye to the birds, and from now on it's strictly work and fight."

For once I wonder if I too am about to regret the parting of the ways. Leaving Tina has been a sore wrench - so sore that only my rigid naval training has enabled me to suppress unhealthy thoughts about desertion. In my wallet is her photo in sepia, but attractive as it is, it cannot do justice to the honey colouring of this beautiful half-caste who has made the days so happy for me.

Chattoo reminds me of Tippee minus a railway station. It is a depressingly stark little port where the storage godowns cluster round the water's edge in various states of decay, doing their best to shelter the impedimenta of war which they house.

As we are not yet allowed on board ship, we are billeted in a campoo around the inevitable maidan, whereby I am introduced for the first time to tents which are half brick and half canvas, as though the builders ran short of cement early on and had to finish off with fabric.

Honners is chummed with me in a large marquee for two, in

company with the ten servants whom we are entitled to. Everywhere I turn there are servants ghosting about the tent, all apparently busy yet secretly watching one's every movement. If I sit down, the cushion mysteriously arranges itself at my back. If I take out a cigarette, a lighted match supported by dusky fingers appears before my very eyes. If I enter the toilet, a clean towel glides on to the rail behind me. If I suggest a drink to Honners, we are silently surrounded by the complex paraphernalia of the sundowner ritual as though we are in an alcoholic's paradise. It is all very unnerving, especially when the empty glass disappears from my hand, to be replaced refilled like a conjuring trick.

Honners accepts the personal service as routine, declaring that it is merely what he was accustomed to back home at the Hall before the war decimated the family retainers. He asserts airily that he had one rustic flunkey whose sole chore in life was to pull the bell-rope if Honners wanted anything, and to assist him into bed after Hunt Balls.

"You, Peter, and the rest of the Bray-type proletariat, are seeing the last of the glorious days of the old British Raj. As for myself, I accept it as to the manner born," Honners replies in response to my protest that I cannot sleep with a white-eyed chuprassi crouched at my bedside waving a punka to circulate the tent fumes.

However, after a night of hot fitful slumber, I awake quite excited at the prospect that today I am to be shown the Fleet at anchor. Commodore Gooji and Staff assemble on the maidan together with sea-going officers, whence we depart in numerous rickshaws in strict order of seniority. The Commodore is of such bulk that his rickshaw-boy is regularly lifted high into the air, his feet still running, every time the officer leans back to chat with his Aide.

In anticipation I sniff the sultry atmosphere in vain for a whiff of sea, but suddenly our long procession turns into Chattoo Docks - and there ahead lies the ocean. Nevertheless, I note that it is empty of shipping. The Fleet, I assume, is always parked out of sight over the horizon, to be reached only by some incredibly difficult mode of marine transport, such as paddling oneself along on an inflated goatskin.

Honners calls over to me, "Well, Peter, there's the ocean you've been harping on about for weeks. Now what do you think of our Fleet?"

"Sunk?" I suggest resignedly, but Commodore Gooji and Staff are all standing with their backs to the sea and staring inland. By turning round to follow their gaze I observe two small ships lying up a creek in cradles, completely clear of the water. From every part of the hulls and superstructures hang long white cloths, limp in the still air, as if the vessels are waiting to be bandaged.

Commodore Gooji is telling me, "There is your fighting home, Lieutenant Pook, lying proud and defiant up the creek. What a moment of joy for you!

I try to pucker up my features into a transport of bliss but fail miserably. The Commodore is pointing to the nearer of the two little ships. "Behind the *Soonong* at the back is lying her brave sister, the *Assang*. What a spectacle they make in all their battle array, ready to strike fear into the heart of the impudent foe from Nippon; impatient to be tearing at the Achilles heel of the - "

"Where's the Fleet then?" I cut in quickly. Many hands point up the creek to indicate the exact position of the Fleet for my benefit.

Honners whispers at my side, "It's a Fleet of two ships, but do your best to register awe. The godowns along the bund are packed with all the salvage equipment they can't squeeze on board."

Turning to Commodore Gooji, I throw up my hands and

whistle through my teeth in pantomime of unbounded dismay - at the spectacle of armed might. He smiles appreciatively and murmurs something about Armadas and puny man.

"A Fleet of only a couple of tiny tubs?" I whisper to Honners.

"Afraid so, Peter - take it or leave it. My advice is think about the pay and take it."

"But what kind of ships are they? Ferry-boats?"

"Actually, Peter, they're not so dusty - a cross between an escort vessel, a corvette, a frigate, and a tea-clipper. Given a fair wind they can nip along at a steady ten knots under full sail."

"Sails! Did you say sails? Are those the rags hanging down all over the place?"

"Oh, no, Peter - the ships are dressed overall with doolhi shrouds in readiness for the blessing by the Gondahs. They have to bless everything connected with the voyage, but particularly the push-along punka, the which-way oar, the boom-boom, and of course, the hubble-bubble suit."

I look straight at Honners but his face is absolutely solemn.

"In case you're not yet familiar with the Ramsami technical terms, Peter, that means the propeller, the rudder, the gun, and the diving-dress," he explains patronizingly.

I look across to Commander Bray for moral support but the Commander is sitting on a bollard, arms folded, eyes closed, in pensive mood, rather like a fakir who endures earthly life by contemplating eternity. Gazing hypnotically at the scene, I perceive numerous white-robed Gondahs circulating round the decks of the *Soonong* at all levels, and a flat chanting rhythm registers in my ears. Honners too notices the movements.

"Peter, it's started at last," he cries excitedly. "Ahoy there, Commander Bray, wake up! The ceremony has begun. The Gondahs are in procession round the *Soonong*."

Opening his bloodshot eyes, Commander Bray surveys the

scene with utter disinterest. "No comment," he grunts bitterly, just as Commodore Gooji addresses us.

"Gentlemen, good news! The Festival of Toolu has commenced and the Gondahs are already singing the Leedees prior to blessing the Fleet with coconut-oil. Therefore let us hurry to the bund that we may witness the historic ceremony without delay, for our Admiral of the Fleet the Nawab of Ramsam is due any minute in person, This way, gentlemen, to see Mars, the god of war, don his fearful armour, as the Romans had it."

A voice says, "Drop dead, mate," but we pretend not to hear it in case it has come from Commander Bray. Instead we form an expectant queue behind the Commodore. It seems that the reference to coconut-oil has had a deleterious effect on commander Bray, who joins the end of the queue mouthing oaths pertaining to the sticky properties of this oil on his decks.

On the jetty the Royal Ramsami Railway Works Band is already in full blast as we file on to the dais to await the arrival of the Nawab. Noticing that Honners is standing to attention with his fingers blocking both ears, I do likewise, under the impression that this is the conventional stance anywhere near the band, but Honners shouts something to the effect that the Nawab is entitled to a nineteen-gun salute and that his entry will coincide with a localized box-barrage.

Without putting too fine a point on it, the arrival of the Nawab is nothing short of terrifying. The whole area erupts in explosions which seem to come from behind the godowns, and momentarily I wonder if we are the victims of a surprise Japanese air-raid. The dais rocks under us, and one of the godowns slowly collapses in a roar of dust and rubble.

"Lie flat, Peter!" Honners screams up at me, so I fling myself down among the prostrate officers - to find myself alongside the

Nawab. Even in the horizontal position he still retains his royal dignity.

"Surprise air-attack, sir!" I shout above the thunder.

"No, Lieutenant Pook - only my official salute. Five more eruptions and it will all be over. Let us pray the dais will hold up under us. Mark my words, there will be an Inquiry into this lamentable affair this very day. Our Army is justifiably jealous of our Navy and they delight in this kind of childish revenge. Heads will fall before sunset, I assure you."

At the conclusion of the Royal Salute we regain our feet and brush off the dust which has arisen from the collapsed warehouse. Commodore Gooji is hopping mad, demanding to know who authorized the setting up of the howitzers so near the dais, yet concealed by the godowns. He is demanding the death penalty for every officer in the Army, and the absorption of that Service by the Navy. He is convinced that the godown has been hit by a live shell intended for us, and pleads with the Nawab to place the whole matter of Royal Salutes in his own capable hands.

"We forbid aeroplanes because they make so much noise yet we put up with this thunder of hell every time our beloved Nawab appears," he cries emotionally. "It almost makes one dread his royal visits. What is more, my Staff Officer has fainted away and the Gondahs have taken to the hills."

He is right, because on the far side of the creek we can discern white-robed figures streaming up the slopes of a ghat, some of whom are carrying the limp forms of less hardy colleagues.

The only calm person in sight is Commander Bray, who stands at the rear of the dais contemplating the ocean in silent resignation.

"He's been compelled to resort to sedative tablets ever since his last trip down to Chattoo," Honners explains in my ear. "He became violent at Chukkoo and got an official reprimand."

Peons are despatched to recall the Gondahs and the Railway Band members from the hills, while various Aides go off in search of the Army officers in charge of the howitzers. Meantime Honners and I survey the salvage stores which have been laid bare by the collapse of the godown.

"Don't take it too badly, Peter," Honners advises me. "These little setbacks happen in the best of businesses. After all, the *Soonong* will soon be shipshape and Bristol fashion."

"But will she ever float?"

"Of course she will. Then you'll find she's not such a bad tub at all. About 1,200 tons, powered by the most modern coal-burning plant imaginable, and you'll be surprised how much difference the sails make when the wind's fair. Admittedly she's a bit cramped, with 200 personnel on board instead of 80 - rather like living in a slum, but that's the price of full employment. Anyhow, you'll soon shake down and grow to love her. Just wait till you see your very own cabin."

This last remark gives me a mental flash of a mud-hut fitted with a porthole, but I say nothing because it is now sundown and the ceremony begins in earnest. The afternoon having been long enough for the Gondahs to get through chanting the Leedees, we all file down on the beach beneath the *Soonong* for the blessing of the push-along punka and the which-way oar. Then we reassemble on deck for the blessing of the boom-boom and the hubble-bubble suit.

The Gondahs conduct an interminable ceremony of ritual and prayer over every item in sight including the toilets, until there appears to be nothing which is not well oiled up. I cannot help noticing how the eyes in Commander Bray's red face roll distractedly as the helm is liberally sprinkled with oil by the Great Gondah, or how the Commander occasionally applies a handkerchief to his cheeks as though he is attending a funeral.

As the moon rises over the mizzen-mast Commodore Gooji and his Aides retire, leaving only Commander Bray and his ship's officers on the quarter-deck.

"It's our turn now," Honners whispers apprehensively.

"What happens? Do they break a bottle of magga across our beads and send us down the slipway?"

"I don't know - this is new ground for me. Better watch Lieutenant Kala - he's a Ramsami who's been to sea once, long before the war. You've probably noticed he's wearing the Ramsami Star for leaving harbour."

Lieutenant Kala nods across to us, then he kneels down, placing his forehead on the deck, so we do likewise. Meanwhile the Gondahs fumble about a bit for the right note prior to moaning a high-pitched dirge. When all are in the same key, they shuffle round and round us and I have to suppress a feeling that I am about to be kicked in the backside. The whole thing is so ridiculous that I want to laugh aloud, but nearby I can just make out Commander Bray's bald pate resting on the deck so I decide to go along with it to avoid trouble.

"They're invoking Toolu to keep the *Soonong* afloat," Honners whispers as he picks up the drift of the chanting. "May she have a safe, prosperous voyage . . . may Commander Bray be inspired by Pijee in his handling of the which-way stick that he can find that which is lost. . . . This is your bit, Peter - may the human crab in the hubble-bubble suit be guided to that which is lying on the sea-bed awaiting recovery . . . . "

"Are they singing anything about getting the *Soonong* waterborne for a start?" I inquire, "or is there any mention of us standing up before the blood goes to my. . . ? I am silenced by a spray of oil on my neck and ears as a Gondah whisks his blesser down smartly in my direction.

"You're being blessed, Peter," Honners tells me. I am

indeed, for the Gondah lifts my head from the deck, flicks the blesser right between my eyes, then replaces my face on the planks. I don't savour the contemptuous way he does it, so I make a mental note of his features for future reference. His sneering lips reveal a missing tooth, which sets up a train of thought in my mind somewhat inconsistent with religious aims.

Eventually the Gondahs seem satisfied that we have been sufficiently blessed, for Commodore Gooji reappears to usher us off the ship with unaccustomed speed. "Hurry please, hurry ashore, gentlemen," he cries urgently, as though the *Soonong* has caught fire. All the while he keeps looking over his shoulder at the range of hills to the north.

"Toolu's Anchor has appeared above the Shaggapore Ghats, so we have to beat it off the ship as quickly as possible," Honners explains, pushing me down the gangplank at the trot. Far behind me I hear Commander Bray shouting and swearing as the Gondahs usher him off his quarter-deck with panic haste.

Concerned, Honners calls aloft, "Abandon ship, Commander Bray, and keep calm! Toolu's Anchor is rising over the Shaggapore Ghats. Hurry up for heaven's sake."

I keep peering northwards for a sight of anything resembling an anchor but can see nothing. Nevertheless, Honners seems so agitated by what I can't spot that we all slither down the oily gangplank to the jetty.

"Whew - that was a close shave!" he gasps as we wipe coconut-oil from our hands and uniforms. "Thank goodness Bray saw reason and followed us."

Our Commander is now sliding along the gangplank, covered in oil, wild-eyed, his great fists thumping the rail as he calls upon his own sea-gods to swallow up all Gondahs and let him sail away for ever while he is yet in command of his faculties.

"Bray is ruining his chances of promotion, carrying on like that," Honners observes worriedly. "Why, it's enough to make him lose his brass hat and be beached on half pay."

"But what's he done wrong?"

"Done wrong? Trying to stay on board when Toolu's Anchor is rising over the . . ." We are interrupted by the passing of Commodore Gooji himself, who has his arm round the skipper's broad shoulders in an effort to pacify him and curtail his views on Gondahs in general. To reinforce his advice, the Commodore points agitatedly to the northern horizon but this merely increases Bray's fury. His earthy nautical language fills the night, and seems far removed from the religious atmosphere of the occasion.

"Honestly, Peter, this is worse than the Chukkoo episode when he got an official reprimand. He's simply throwing discipline to pot."

"What is all this nonsense about an anchor appearing over a hill, that's what I want to know? "

"Oh, thought you were in the picture, Peter. *We* call it the Great Bear Constellation or the Plough, but to the Ramsamis it's Toolu's Anachor. No one except the Gondahs is allowed to stay on board when it rises during the Festival, particularly foreign devils like us."

"That's all very well, but what are we supposed to do if we were at sea - jump overboard?"

"Good gracious no, Peter. The resident Gondah gives us special dispensation to remain aboard, but we have to hide in our cabins. Otherwise the link between Pijee and Mother Earth would be broken, and then - *bloop* - down goes your ship like an iron mangle."

"If you don't mind my saying so, you seem to have learnt an awful lot for your age, Honners. How come you're such a little know-all about Pijee-lore?"

"I *read,* Peter," Honners explains in a tone implying that others would do well to follow his example. "You see, I hope to park in this mob permanently after the war because the back-to-nature atmosphere and the Eastern culture appeal to the aesthetic qualities in me. Also I prefer 15,000 rupees a year to 2s. 3d. a day in the Marines - remember?"

"All right, Honners, every man to his own taste. One thing though, now the blessings are over I figure we should be at sea just as soon as they can carry the *Soonong* down to the water's edge and push her clear of the bunder - that thought makes me feel a whole lot better."

Henners' face clouds over. "Not so fast, Peter. Haven't you had a chitty from the Commodore about our embarkation leave?"

"Embarkation leave! You're joking, surely? We've had nothing else ever since we arrived in Ramsam."

"Oh, you're not allowed to put to sea without your leave, Peter - it's laid down in Orders. Here's my chitty, so you can read it for yourself. We've clicked for the full entitlement of twelve weeks."

This news sets me back to the extent that I am struck dumb, and a feeling of utter despair wells over me. Subconsciously I wonder what this new delay will do to our skipper but my mind hastily rejects the answer. At length I say to my friend, "Where are you going to spend your leave, Honners - home in England? I suppose I could come back with you and take a temporary job in London."

"Oh, no, Peter, we're not allowed to leave the country in time of war. I was going to suggest we return to Shaggapore for a while, then go up to Jawanagar to cool off in the hills. Of course, we'll take the girls with us. Everybody who's anybody quits Shaggapore during the Shilla -that's the hot season - so we shan't go short of company. In any case, that's what we have to do. It's in Orders."

My mind forms the theory that Honners must be a Ramsami albino.

FIVE

It seems rather strange to be back at Jawanagar again, staying once more in the Hotel Republique opposite N.H.Q. in the company of everybody we met at Shaggapore. In fact we travelled up the line to Tippee, changed trains, and continued on to Jawanagar like a giant works outing for everybody we ever knew in Ramsam.

Commander Bray's appeal for permission to spend a sailing holiday around Chattoo harbour in order to bring back memories of his maritime profession has been turned down on the grounds that technically this would involve leaving the country. For the same reason I have been refused leave to climb in the vicinity of Mount Everest with my friends, and the refusal has contained the rider that mountaineering is considered to be a most unsuitable pursuit for a naval officer.

However, as a special concession we are all ordered to Baada, a hill station 8,000 feet up in the Ghats, where the cool days and frosty nights will thicken our blood and take us clear of the malarial districts below. Baada is reached by a single-track line from Jawanagar, which winds its way round the mountains until one has the interesting experience of looking out of the compartment window at the clouds below. The passengers exploit the situation of travelling in a train above the clouds to the full, by pointing downwards at the clouds and saying, "Looks like rain again," and a dozen other witticisms inspired by the unusual.

But when a Major Talbot persists by thinking he sees a storm brewing underfoot, Honners sniffs loudly and asks the Major if he writes those banal jokes one finds in Christmas crackers. The journey continues in silence.

At Baada, our hotel goes under the nostalgic name of Grassmere Lake Rest House, and indeed the scenery is reminiscent of its namesake. In front of the hotel is a large lake, full of reeds and small terrapins. As we have strict instructions that this is a sacred lake, completely taboo and a death-trap to human life, Honners and I decide that we will swim across it the very first moonless night which offers.

Meanwhile we go horse-riding, play tennis, and indulge in the standard pursuits on which Britons abroad rely in order to overcome the handicap of not being allowed to work in a foreign land. As one would expect under these circumstances every ear is open like aircraft-detectors to catch the slightest breath of scandal, and every tongue is poised either to transmit it or invent it.

The combination of climate, rich food, drink, and that superfluity of servants which makes an active person soon feel like an invalid seeking occupational-therapy, has the most stimulating effect on both sexes, so that the matrimonial tangles rapidly develop beyond immediate unravelling. The Operations-Room for the gossip war is undoubtedly the lounge of our hotel, where the ladies, led by Mrs. Smith, plan their campaigns over the bridge tables with the thoroughness of Generals in the field.

There is only one other body of experts who know more than these ladies, and they reside in the servants' quarters.

Sensing that the ladies are flogging the current scandals to death, and are quite desperate for fresh material to relieve hill station ennui, I encourage the rumour that when the Nawabani danced with me at the Grand Mobilization Ball it was no mere gesture of courtesy. In addition I take pains to let it be known at different times that I am in love with most women at the hotel, including Mrs. Smith's daughter, Peggy.

Powerful Peg, as I affectionately call her, is one of those rare girls who could crew on a merchant ship in perfect safety. In fact, her frequent glances reduce me to a state of utter sexlessness. Powerful Peg's passion is horse-riding. At all hours of the day her large posterior is to be seen delineated in jodhpurs as she wobbles to the stables in search of another thin-legged animal which will cart her across Ramsam. It is noticeable that her companions are periodically brought back to the hotel on stretchers, suffering from broken collarbones, concussion, and suchlike rewards of the sport. But not so Peggy. Every evening she returns with a ruddy complexion and loud voice, whacking her riding-boots with a crop as she organizes the party for tomorrow's hunt.

Her mother has already declared it is high time she took a husband, hinting that I am the only man in the hotel young enough to be one and robust enough to cope with the bride. Hence I am obliged to start another rumour, via Honners, that alimony is being deducted monthly from my pay-chit.

As for Honners - he throws himself heart and soul into the role of promiscuous lover by creeping about the hotel by night, clad in a dressing-gown and ogling everyone in sight including the redoubtable Mrs. Smith herself. As usual he overdoes the whole business, and much to his annoyance is earmarked by the ladies as a cute little fellow, totally incapable of vice, and the one unblemished character in the hotel. Of course, this high esteem has nothing to do with Mrs. Smith's unbounded joy concerning his ancient family title.

So completely do the husbands trust Honners that they go out of their way at night to meet him in the corridors for the purpose of guiding him to the bathroom, being under the impression that he is one of those simple souls who become lost in the ramifications of large hotels. As he puts it himself, "It's damned hard work trying to be lecherous when everybody thinks you've got a weak bladder and no sense of direction."

Commander Bray is utterly aloof from all gossip, passing the time sitting by the lake and reading *Sailing Alone around the World* by Captain Joshua Slocum, aloud to Rana. He and Rana have long since run out of conversation with each other, partly because his thoughts are usually far out in the Pacific with Captain Slocum on board the *Spray,* and partly because Rana's mind is of remarkably small capacity, to be probed as one would a winkle with a pin.

When the Commander tires of reading aloud he looks at the water of the lake with that blank hopeless stare of an Englishman on holiday waiting for the next meal. Every morning at breakfast, when the wobbly wives with big handbags descend in voracious columns, Commander Bray ostentatiously pencils through the date on the wall-calendar next to the hotel barometer as though he is in jail.

We have come to dread the dining-room as much as the lounge, where we can never overcome our surprise at the food consumption of the guests, who could not eat more if they were on shift-work in a quarry.

"Don't you think there is something inferior about other people, Peter?" Honners asks me in a loud voice over the papaya course. "Especially when they persist in the naive humour of the holiday-camp social."

This remark has been inspired by Mrs. Smith's standard morning gambit to Honners: "And how is our naughty little lover-boy this morning, eh? Not too tired, we hope."

"Don't take all the honey again," Honners replies coldly. "The bees are fed up with it."

Already we have noted the high percentage of diabetics among the diners, averaging almost one to a table. Their lives are dictated by pills and special dishes, which supply much needed material for table smalltalk because each item must be checked for ingredients before it is accepted. Consequently they devour everything in sight except the sugar-bowl.

The tenor of our lives so changes that we are in a fever of excitement at the prospect of the first night frost. Mrs. Smith recalls the winter of '23 when experienced observers reported the fall of a snowflake on the stoep of the hotel. As a precaution against a recurrence of '23 she is at present engaged in knitting a pullover like a life-jacket to protect her frail husband from the elements when he passes from the letter-rack to the bar.

Tension mounts as numerous bearers prepare the fireplaces for lighting at the first hint of mild weather. We gather round like retarded children to witness the miracle of combustion in the grate. "Just fancy - a real old English fire," croons Mrs. Smith ecstatically. "You boys little dreamed you'd ever see one of those out here in Ramsam, I'll wager a cockney's barrow."

Honners winces visibly at Mrs. Smith's attempt to remind us of Home and Blighty. The rest of us make polite surprise noises, except Commander Bray who mutters something about burning the lot of you if I had my way.

"Will smoke really come out and go up the chimney?" I inquire, trying to appear enthralled.

"Yes indeed, dear boy, and then - believe it or not - hot muffins and tea around the hearth for all of us, just like being back in dear old Blighty. My daughter Peggy will see *you* don't go short, Peter."

A general hubbub of nostalgia and anticipation wells up from the guests, turning the conversation to London fogs, kippers, pubs, burst pipes, hot chestnuts, yule-logs, Piccadilly, and all the stock thorns of remembrance with which Britons torment themselves when they are on to a good thing in a foreign land and don't have to go back home.

"Oh, quickly everyone - turn on the radio. In our excitement we nearly forgot the News," cries Mrs. Smith, holding up both hands in horror. Her husband flings himself Commando-fashion across the lounge to the radio and switches on nervously. Part of our war-effort is to listen to all News bulletins from London as though we are members of an Underground Movement awaiting orders.

Sometimes the News comes through so loudly that the windows rattle, while at other times one of us has to press his ear to the speaker and relay the tidings, sentence by sentence, to the expectant patriots behind. If the News is good we cheer. If bad, we groan and wish we were back Home to suffer with our fellow countrymen.

At the conclusion of each News Commodore Gooji alters little pins on the wall-map of the lounge to indicate the latest strategic moves on the world battlefronts, while Miss Talbot chalks the headlines on a blackboard set up beside it.

Commodore Gooji personally lectures us on strategy and explains where the Allied Navies are going wrong. The land campaigns are in the capable hands of Major Talbot (Retired), late of the Pay Corps. The Allied Air Forces come under the direct supervision of Miss Talbot, dauntless sister of the Major, whose zeal for the Allied cause has led her to write to the B.B.C. complaining of the grammatical error of verb in their statement that "None of our aircraft are missing." The entire Grand Strategy of the war is coordinated by Mrs. Smith, who devours every News as intensely as she does the hotel food.

Between each News we often tune in to Radio Ramsam because most of its entertainers are known to us personally, such as Miss Talbot who accompanies her own singing on the piano, and whose constant rendering of "Keep the Home Fires Burning" is beginning to evoke disturbing psychological impulses in our minds as to the suitability of Miss Talbot as fuel for this commendable purpose.

Another regular broadcaster is Mrs. Smith with her Housewives' Hour every Monday. She gives recipes for little dinner-parties for thirty people without using sugar, and explains how to carry on in the home when seven or eight servants are down with beriberi.

Every Friday Commodore Gooji broadcasts his weekly survey of the war in English and Ramsami, during which he demands that the struggle be prosecuted with renewed vigour by the Free World until the Lion of Liberty has ground the Tiger of Tyranny to powder, etcetera. His oration is always followed by stirring Ramsami music of such pitch and vehemence - like massed bagpipers in revolt - that it strikes terror in the hearts of friend and foe alike.

Every Saturday night we hold the Victory Ball in the hotel lounge, where we dance to the music of Miss Talbot (piano) and Mr. Smith (drum). This event begins in cold blood with duty dances all round for the benefit of our more elderly female patriots, but as the magga and whisky flow freely so the dance warms up, until it becomes a refined orgy of banter and close embraces.

All this is noted in Mrs. Smith's camera-like memory, to be offered in evidence at Sunday's tea session. By eleven o'clock, Mr. Smith steels himself to desert the drum and dance with anybody in sight who is not his wife. Precisely at midnight Miss Talbot thumps out the National Anthem with histrionic violence, which is our cue to stand to attention and implore Providence at the top of our voices to rescue the King, as though he is trapped in a burning building while we stand powerless below.

After the Victory Ball the younger set often defy convention by holding a bottle-party in someone's bedroom, and it is under these exhilarating conditions that Honners and I decide to swim across the sacred lake of Baada. Everybody else backs out on the grounds either that they are poor swimmers or that there may be something in this taboo after all. Wagers are laid against our success, and the girls walk round to the opposite shore of the lake to guide us by holding flashlights to mark our destination.

"Everybody must keep absolutely silent," Honners warns us as I undress, "because if Gooji gets to hear of it he'll have the Gondahs down on our heads for defiling Pijee's Drinking-Bowl or whatever they call the lake."

As Honners and I walk into the water through the shiny mud we are surprised at the coldness of it. Honners shudders aloud when he ducks his shoulders, and even louder when a terrapin scuttles out of his way. I strike out with the crawl, while Honners settles down to a steady side-stroke. In truth we are not too happy about Honners making this trip because it is only recently that he has learned to swim at all, but he has never yet been put off doing what he has set his mind to. Just to be on the safe side I let him make the pace, keeping close behind in case of trouble.

A surprisingly large number of terrapins slide about our bodies, and the darkness does nothing to boost our morale, but, worst of all, the reeds impede our feet all the time.

"It's like swimming over a flooded wheat-field," Honners calls to me. "I guess we'll have a short blow on the island."

This island, about the size of a football pitch, is pretty well plumb in the centre of the lake, and tradition says no one has ever been on it except Toolu back in the year dot. Swimming along in this black water makes all the strange Ramsami beliefs seem far more plausible than they did in the warm lighted bar of the hotel, especially now that we can see Toolu's Anchor standing up on the northern horizon like a giant pylon of stars watching our exploit.

"All I can say is, let's hope Toolu doesn't complain to his

brother Pijee about us being out here in his blessed drinking-bowl," Honners gasps, "because I sure can do with a rest on his little island."

"Steady she goes, Honners. Another few yards and we're there."

Now my eyes have grown accustomed to the dark I can distinguish the outline of palm-trees on the islet. Also I notice that the weeds are thickening. So thick in fact that one hardly knows whether to go on swimming or get up and walk. Our arrival seems to be disturbing a nature reserve, for the fish and terrapins are plopping all around us as we half scramble over the reeds and reach the islet. Honners says quietly, "Sorry, Peter, but I'm all in. Pull me up as soon as you can."

I am doing my best, but getting on the islet is no easy task. It is so choked with undergrowth, trees, and thorny bushes that the best I can do is to press my body forward into the foliage until I have claimed sufficient ground to stand on. Directly I am established I heave Honners inboard by his arm, then let him recover for a few minutes.

"Let's edge round the island so we can spot the flashlights on the far bank of the lake," I suggest after an interval.

"Then you go first, Peter, because I can't see in the dark. What's more, I don't like these noises everywhere."

Nor do I. The undergrowth seems alive with invisible creatures scampering and hissing through it, while overhead flying-foxes are quitting the palm-trees at the sound of our voices. The overhanging bushes make it impossible to circumnavigate the islet but fortunately we locate a break in the undergrowth which allows us to push inland, as it were, along a narrow path like a rabbit-run.

"This is probably a track made by iguana lizards," Honners decides gloomily, "so let's cross as fast as sin and hit the water for the last lap. Believe me, from now on I'm a strict Pijee disciple if he'll only let me get out of this lot in one . . . Peter, there's a leopard ahead!

We shall never know what species of beast owns the two luminous eyes which shine in our direction because we run along the track until we are brought to a standstill by a large wooden obstruction. It seems we have stumbled across a hut of some kind, about eight feet square, no windows, and a padlocked door.

"What on earth is a hut doing on Toolu's Island where no man has trod before?" I ask puzzledly, but Honners does not reply. Instead, he points fearfully at the low roof. This time there is no mistaking that we have company in the shape of snake oozing along the shingles of the roof. You can't fail to recognize a python, particularly the netted python of Indo-China, when there's twenty-five feet of fat coils building up within touching distance, giving one the impression that the roof is a living mass.

Simultaneously our bodies jet forward, not stopping till we hit the water on the far side. Without a word we strike out for the two dots of light visible ashore.

Honners is progressing so swiftly with his side-stroke that it is all I can do to keep abreast of him. "Take it easy, Honners," I warn him. "It's a long way to go, so don't burn yourself out."

"Swim for your life, Peter. Don't bother about me -save yourself if you can."

His progress is punctuated by gasps of revulsion as various forms of marine life graze our bodies, some silky soft, some slimy, all hideous to our tense nerves. A kind of hairy crab seems intent on driving me insane by repeatedly scuttling across my back and plopping into the water on the other side.

Now the weeds thicken again, so I estimate we are nearing the far shore of the lake. But this time they become so matted and clinging that we can swim no further.

"Feels like we're trapped in the Sargasso Sea, Honners," I shout to my friend.

"I'm done for, Peter," he gasps back. "Toolu has won all right. What a damn-fool mess to get ourselves into. Any chance of giving me a hand?" Honners says this so quietly and calmly that I know he is in a bad way. Thinking quickly, I figure there is no time to bring help from shore, even supposing any is available. On the other hand it seems I shall need all my strength to get there myself, let alone help Honners. Nevertheless, something has to be done fast.

"Float on your back, pal, and don't panic," I order him.

"The Pilkington-Goldbergs are not in the habit of panicking," he replies, turning over exhausted. "Tradition requires them to drown tight-lipped."

Now I position myself ahead of Honners, grab his hair in my left hand, and try to tow him along through the reeds. By closing my eyes and paddling with my free arm we inch forward, but how far is impossible to gauge in the darkness.

Honners tries to help by threshing his feet feebly while I make a quick calculation that the flashlights seem to be about a hundred yards off.

But now we are really in trouble because, although I don't tell Honners, I can no longer spare my left hand to keep him afloat if I am to save myself. It has already gone numb, and Honners' hair slips from it like wet seaweed. Slowly my friend sinks below the surface of the lake without a sound whilst I watch helplessly. In fact, all I can do is float on my back in the hope that enough strength will return to me for renewed effort. I try calling for help but nothing emerges except a hoarse croak.

Subconsciously I wonder if this cold lake really has a curse on it, with the power to engulf all who intrude there. I ask myself is it possible that my long friendship with Honners through so many of the world's battle-zones is to end like this in a senseless midnight escapade. The dead-weight of despair grips my shivering body.

"Stand up, Peter, it's all right here - only about five feet deep," a voice says nearby. "Push down on the reeds with your feet and you can touch bottom."

Although a flashlight is blinding my eyes I recognize the gruff tone of Commander Bray. "Thank God you've come, Commander," I cry thankfully, "but Honners has gone under. Only a minute ago - we may still be able to locate him with the light." So saying, I push my feet through the reeds and encounter the muddy bottom.

Commander Bray helps me stand upright. "Don't worry about Honners," he grunts, "I've got him high and dry. Exhausted and waterlogged, but all in one piece."

"Where?"

"Up here."

The glow of the torch shows me Honners' body lying round the Commander's great shoulders like a scarf.

"It's true, Peter," the body confirms feebly. "Thought I was a goner but here I am - half dead."

This news makes me feel so happy that I forget my fatigue and the strange creatures scuttling over my feet on the lake bed. If I had the strength I'd cheer at the top of my voice.

"All we have to do now is to wade back through this muck of weeds as best we can," Commander Bray advises us. "I'll carry Honners while you go in front, Peter, so I can keep an eye on you. We won't worry about the court martial till tomorrow, eh?"

The knowledge that Honners is all right is so good for my soul that I don't care what happens tomorrow. Besides, I need every ounce of strength and concentration to stagger through the rushes.

Characteristically, Commander Bray puts us in the picture *en route*. "I strolled out on the hotel balcony for a cigar and saw two lights glimming across the lake," he explains, "so, being bored stiff as usual, I decided to walk round the shore for a look-see and security check. Eventually I caught up with the girls, who were pretty anxious about the delay in your arrival. We heard voices and splashing, then I spotted you by the phosphorescent glow you stirred up in the water. Just to be on the safe side I waded out, and more by luck than judgement I barged into Honners - a very *passé* Honners at that."

Both of us recover quickly from the ordeal, but unfortunately there is no hiding the whole stupid business from the residents. In fact a large party headed by Mrs. Smith is waiting in the foyer, agog for news. Miss Talbot declares that nothing comparable has hit Baada since '27, when a rogue elephant walked across the croquet lawn and tried to enter the lounge via the french-windows. She is corrected by an incredibly ancient lady who bears a striking resemblance to a parrot wearing ear-rings. She cites the unaccountable pregnancy of a Miss Brown, following a tiger shikari in '98 led by a certain Colonel Robinson.

Commodore Gooji is rushing about in anguish as he receives the full report in dribs and drabs. Only he, it appears, perceives the full implication of what has taken place. Soon, he warns, the Gondahs will be demanding punishment for those who have violated Toolu's Drinking-Bowl and set foot on Pijee's Stepping Stone. The repercussions could well lead to the acute embarrasment of the Nawab - even to the fall of the Government itself.

Hurried conferences are being held behind locked doors by the Commodore and his Aides before a definite plan of action is decided upon. This is promulgated at seven o'clock in the morning, directly it has been approved by the Nawab over the phone, and it contains three main sections.

Part One involves Honners and me being put on the train for Jawanagar under close arrest. Part Two states that all naval leave is cancelled as from now; all ranks to report to Chattoo under immediate sailing orders. Part Three, hints that a full Inquiry into the affair will be held as soon as all parties are available.

"Gooji is a shrewd old bird," Commander Bray comments when he hears the news. "Pipe all hands to sea, and then promise an Inquiry in the distant future when things have blown over somewhat. Pretty sharp diplomacy, if you ask me.

"But what about Honners and me? How can you sail without the humancrab?" I demand indignantly.

"Ah, Peter, don't worry about that; you'll be on board all right - then you can tell me more about that hut you spotted on Toolu's Island."

"Oh, that! Probably some old religious tool-shed or something, I guess."

"What? - with a radio aerial sticking up through the roof?" Honners cuts in emphatically. "That python so took my mind off things that I didn't give the aerial much attention."

Commander Bray looks serious. "Don't mention it to a soul, understand? At the first opportunity we'll have a conflab about it, then I'll decide what action to take from the security angle."

At the moment I have absolutely no interest in tool-sheds, with or without aerials. What is worrying me is the prospect of being jailed at Jawanagar while the *Soonong* could well judder out to sea without me.

Commander Bray dismisses my fears with a wave of his large fist. "Nothing to it, Peter. You won't be detained more than hours - then it's all change at Tippee as fast as we can make it. I can forgive you anything now that you've managed to get this endless leave cut short, and then - Ahoy there! Weigh anchor! Cast off for'ard! We put to sea at last."

"But what do they want with Honners and me at Jawanagar?" I persist. "Statements, finger-prints, and all that malarky?"

Commander Bray throws back his head and bellows noisily. "No, lad - that'll come later. At the moment you're to see Surgeon Rear-Admiral Kappatta at N.H.Q., where you're due for just about every anti-whatnot injection in his locker. They tell me half the sewage of Baada finds its way into that lake you wallowed in."

SIX

As Commander Bray predicted, we receive every injection in the book at Jawanagar Hospital except the long needle for rabies. Dr. Kappatta and his students are so delighted to have a couple of walking cesspools in the ward to experiment on that we reverse the usual procedure with patients by entering the hospital quite fit and departing half dead.

Consequently Honners and I remember little of the journey down to Chattoo Harbour, travelling in a kind of feverish coma punctuated by bouts of fear as the implications of our swim permeate our weary minds. Mostly we live on aspirins washed down with rum and lime-juice - a certain antidote for all tropical ills, Commander Bray assures us - with the result that every time I look at Tina I groan sadly, for physiological reasons of a personal nature.

Shrini has to nurse Honners by holding the lime-juice to his lips since he has lost the use of both arms. The injections and vaccination have taken so well that his sleeves contain limbs which are little better than swollen bladders of pain, locked fast at the joints. In a moment of jest he observes that he can salute only by placing his head in his lap.

For once the length of the journey serves a useful purpose because by the time we reach Chattoo, having said farewell to the girls at Chukkoo, our constitutions are on the mend, much to Honners' surprise, for he has been confidently predicting at Tippee that the Gondahs can have his body for ceremonial rites associated with retribution.

It is indeed a memorable day when Commander Bray stands on the bridge of the *Soonong,* surveying the seemingly endless procession climbing the gangplank prior to sailing time.

"I estimate we have 800 souls aboard," he confides to me. "That is to say, 200 crew members and 600 relatives seeing them off."

"Reminds you of Navy Week at Pompey," I muse, idly plucking at the five flower-garlands hung round my neck by the official Ramsami Farewell Deputation. As Captain of the ship, Commander Bray received seven garlands, which give him the appearance of being part of a floral tableau, but we have been advised not to remove them until well clear of the harbour.

Eventually the ship's bell rings an urgent staccato, to indicate that the visitors are requested to stop spitting betel-juice all over our decks and retire to the jetty. It takes us an hour and a half to clear the ship because every time the visitors are ushered off, the crew go with them. When the crew are coaxed aboard again, they bring back their relatives in droves.

Ultimately Commander Bray solves the problem by clearing the ship, mustering the crew on the jetty, and then personally checking them up the gangway. By now the decks resemble the Chelsea Flower Show as the crew shuffle on board laden with garlands, but our skipper can wait no longer. Casting off fore and aft, we slowly ease away from the jetty as the rowers in the towing-dhoneys pull on their oars to the rhythm of traditional Ramsami towing chants.

These songs go something like this: "Yuhumi, humi, humi, humi, *ungar!*" At the word *ungar* the rowers jerk the oars some five inches through the water, causing the ropes to tauten and pull the dhoneys back to the *Soonong.* It is all so ineffectual that the ship drifts with the ebb tide away from the shore.

"What a disgusting shambles!" Commander Bray swears from the bridge. "All those dhoneys do is make us drift out of harbour stern first. Lieutenant Pook, speak below and see if there is any hope of assistance from the engine-room."

I inquire into the voice-pipe, to be greeted by an interminable saga from the other end delivered in Ramsami. "You have a go," I tell Honners. My friend listens to the voice-pipe for a long time, then he interprets the reply. "Very sorry, Sahib, but the push-along punka is not turning because fire very sleepy. Water in boiler is lazy fellow. Outside harbour is blowing good Pijee breeze, so we must be hoisting sails until fire wake up and make water in boiler very angry. Aye, aye, Sahib."

For a moment I fear Commander Bray is about to have a fit standing up, but he pulls himself together and wipes his brow. "If you hadn't heard that twaddle for yourself you wouldn't believe anyone'd have the gall to send up such monkey talk to the bridge, would you? Twenty-odd stokers - and the fire's gone bye-byes. Pook, go below and tell the Chief I want a head of steam by sundown, even if he has to use a gas-poker to raise it. Honners, pipe all hands on deck and see to it that sails are spread on the fore, main, and mizzen masts - every stitch including the big spinnaker for'ard. I'm warning you, if we fail to make the open sea on this tide we'll be recalled for a refit in dry-dock - and that'll mean at least two years by what I've seen of Chattoo Dockyard."

By now the current is taking the *Soonong* towards the harbour mouth, despite the efforts of the towing-dhoneys which seem bent on bringing us back to the jetty.

"Cast off and push off, you useless shower!" Commander Bray thunders through the megaphone at them. "How in hell can a poor devil do anything with that Henley Regatta mob holding our bows to shore all the time?

"How long before the tide turns, sir?" I inquire tactlessly.

"*After* my ship is safely over the bar, don't you fear, Pook. Then life will be tolerable again. Make no mistake, the Hindus are good seamen and the Moslems are first-rate gunners - nothing here which won't improve when we shake down at sea. In port my hands are tied, understand? All we need now is for the Gondah to pipe all hands to prayers and we've had it. Get him up here on the bridge and I'll have him invoke Pijee for more wind - that'll keep his mind occupied - then directly there's some way on the ship we'll use the which-way stick... I mean the helm, of course."

Just at this moment the voice-pipe whistles shrilly. It is the Chief Engineer. "Coal very sleepy, Sahib, so all going to fetch bolloo."

"Good work, Chief," I shout back. "Keep it up and report progress. Are you well stocked for bolloo? Fine. Throw it on ek dum quick - expense no object in a crisis."

Commander Bray jumps on me. "What was that about bolloo, Pook?" he snaps.

"The coal's still sleepy, sir, so they're resorting to bolloo."

"Do you know what bolloo is, man? "

"No, sir. Some kind of quick-burning fuel, I imagine."

"It's tea, you punk! They're standing down for tea and buns - at a time like this. Praise the saints none of my old shipmates can see me in this shambles. Get below, Pook, and tell any man who goes for bolloo that he'll eat it in irons - got me?"

As I hurry below, the sails are creaking up all along the decks to the soulless dirge of traditional Ramsami hoisting chants of Yuhumi, humi, humi, humi, *ungar,* but at least they are halting the *Soonong's* tendency to go astern. With luck Commander Bray may be able to turn her into the off-shore breeze. I pass the ship's Gondah in white robes, waving a great palm-leaf and playing a kind of blow-football with his lips as though he is supplying all the wind we have. Seeing me, he droops his heavy eyelids disdainfully, and I recognize him as the priest who blessed me on the quarter-deck. I exhort him to wave the leaf harder. Anything rather than have him pipe all hands to pray for wind, which presumably involves the entire crew mustering aft and blowing on the sails.

Back on the bridge Commander Bray is using all his seamanship to keep the *Soonong* off the sandbar to the west of the harbour mouth, but despite his efforts she is imperceptibly tacking on to it. Between you and me, although I once told him to his face that he couldn't control a plastic duck in his bath, if he can't do it nobody can - one of the old breed who sniff the wind, eye the clouds, and then come up with the right answer at the precise moment when the radar-happy youngsters are abandoning ship.

Grabbing the voice-pipe, he blares, "Muster whichever watch isn't either praying or having bolloo, and lower the cutters. We'll try to row ourselves clear. Yes, I know it's a stupid idea and likely to entail loss of life - yours for a start - but I want both cutters in the water immediately, if not half-hour sooner."

On receipt of this hazardous order No. 1 cutter descends vertically from the davits, entering the water like a dart to remain standing upright with its nose stuck in the sand.

No. 2 cutter is lowered in more orthodox fashion, whereupon Honners, myself, and a Moslem crew board her and start rowing like robots in an effort to pull the *Soonong* away from the sandbar. Vile language from the rail above informs us that coconut-oil from the blessing ceremony has dried and dogged the running-tackle of the davit, thus fouling No. 1 cutter. The speaker, Commander Bray, personally frees the block with a four-pound hammer, so very shortly that cutter is righted and helping us in our task.

It is exhausting work but there is no doubt that the trick is enabling the *Soonong* to inch out into the channel, clear of the spit. Moreover, the breeze freshens, giving the skipper a chance to bring his helm to our aid.

By sundown the *Soonong* passes out through the narrow mouth of the harbour - caught between wind, tide, and the two cutters. She does not so much sail out as slide sideways in a giant skid, but clear she is, so the cutter crews return on board exhausted.

"Boat stations! All hands to boat stations! Unidentified submarine on the starboard quarter!" comes the unwelcome order from the ship's blower directly the cutters are stowed.

"What the devil's this then?" I demand of Honners as we don life-jackets and hurry to stations. "Barely left harbour and someone's seen a sub already. It's ridiculous."

"The only way to clear the ship, Peter. My job to round up stowaways before we sail - this winkles them out faster than a free grog issue. Twenty-seven assorted wives, relatives, sweethearts to date - not to mention sundry tradesmen. Also it's a good chance for the first boat-drill - nothing like a sub on the starboard quarter for ensuring a smart turn-out, believe me. It's all Bray's idea - I suppose he used to do it with Lord Nelson."

The stowaways emerge on deck in an orgy of surrender, and two or three jump overboard to swim the short distance to the little headland village of Yamala rather than risk being fished by a sub. The rest are put ashore in a cutter while the Commander stands the ship's company down.

"His next move is gunnery practice tomorrow," Honners informs me. "He lets the Moslem laddies play havoc with the artillery, and that takes all the steam out of the Gondah and his pals. In fact we have gunnery most days, just to discourage too many religious ceremonies - except when it's rough, and then we don't have to worry anyway."

About three cables from shore the ship shudders as though she really has been fished by a submarine. Crockery rattles, glasses are thrown about and bulkheads groan, rather like an earth-tremor on land. A mighty throb reverberates through the hull, to be repeated at decreasing intervals. On deck a great cheer arises from the men, many of whom shake hands, embrace, and dance delightedly round the hatches.

Involuntarily I cry, "We've struck a reef!"

"No, Peter, the engine has started up," Honners tells me brightly, as a black roll of smoke belches from the stack. "So the coal has woken up at last and got out of bed. Now water in boiler very angry, eh?"

Commander Bray tugs happily at the fog-horn lanyard as his ship leaps forward, building up a steady seven knots to steam away from the Motherland. Our voyage has started in earnest, I console myself.

To be quite frank, there is little work for me to do on board the *Soonong,* except to unpack and check the brand-new salvage equipment which so many of the Great Powers have kindly contributed to Ramsam. However I do this chore with scrupulous care because it is I alone who will be going down on whatever mission awaits me.

In addition I have to train the Shakalese ratings in the art of diving, mainly in order to comply with R.R. Fleet Order 3705, which states that a spare diver must stand by in case I foul up under water. One can only trust that should this happen, we don't both foul up. As an added precaution Honners has promised to stand by when I am down, lest the ratings decide to desert the pumps half-way through and go for bolloo and buns.

Sailing under secret orders, Commander Bray refuses to discuss anything connected with our course, other than emphasize that navigating the *Soonong* is not the easiest job in the world, akin to steering a barrel, and that should we ever meet with an enemy warship it must be attributed to coincidence rather than design. He adds that officially we are on reconnaissance patrol. Furthermore, he warns us not to make any arrangements for Thursday next because this is Toolu's Birthday; so that, gunnery or no gunnery, it will remind us of the General Strike afloat.

For three days the *Soonong* cruises quietly down the Bay of Bengal while she tries out her teeth and the crew gradually shake down. The watches are organized according to religions, whereby there is nearly always a body of men free to run the ship at any given time. Despite the handicaps of a multi-racial ship, there is much good talent on board. For example, the Moslems soon prove that they are as efficient and accurate on gunnery trials as ever, while the Hindus excel themselves in handling the cumbersome sails with which the *Soonong* is bedevilled.

The ratings allocated to me are Buddhists and Shakalese recruits, young fellows who work hard and pick up my instructions with surprising rapidity. Although they have never seen a diving-pump before, they master its complexities in double quick time, enabling me to form several diving parties each capable of working efficiently and independently. The Petty Officers in particular are intelligent, cheerful, and courageous. Indeed, what higher tribute could be paid to these men than the very fact that they manage to sail and fight such a hybrid creature of the sea as the *Soonong?*

Controlling everything and everybody is the dominating personality of Commander Bray, who runs the ship by an odd, mixture of skill and brute force which overcomes all obstacles. Now we are at sea he has bulged to double his former stature, striding the decks and filling the ocean with his shouts like a baldheaded Captain Bligh in his best hour. He sees the voyage as another challenge of duty, and prepares to carry it through as such. Although he appears not to know it, the men affectionately call him Irumba Bray Sahib - rougly translated as Mr. Volcano.

But volcano or not, even Commander Bray has to lie dormant on Toolu's Birthday, for we are about to celebrate one of the strangest days at sea I have ever witnessed. Actually it begins Wednesday evening when the skipper is ordering sandwiches and a thermos-flask of coffee from the galley and advising us to do likewise.

"Tomorrow the ship dies," he explains dolefully. "No work, no cooking - even the boiler-fires go out. We lie doggo until midnight, when Toolu is reborn. It's the Gondah's big day, so do your best to go along with it. Find a good book and stay in your cabin - or else jump over the side. After the fast comes the feast on Friday when the ship looks like Hempstead Heath on Bank Holiday. Don't try to fight it Peter. Just relax and go with the tide. It's the Ramsami's biggest festival, so all sects have to toe the line. See you Friday."

All that Thursday Honners and I are cabin-bound, trying to read or yarn the time away. Owing to the complete shut-down there are no lights, even candles being taboo. When I smoke a cigarette, Honners stands guard at the door in case the Gondah should smell fire and report us to Bray. The ship is so deathly hushed that I creep along to the toilets mainly with the idea of discovering if the crew have abandoned ship, but I see them lying about the decks motionless as though we have been the victims of a gas attack.

The *Soonong* rides gently at anchor while Commander Bray keeps watch as best he can by peering furtively from his cabin porthole. Every four hours he ghosts along to our cabin for a glass of magga and a whispered chat. "Never mind, lads, it's only once a year," he consoles us. "Anyway, I figured it would be as good a time as any to talk over your little escapade on Toolu's Island. I'm drafting a report on the matter but that shack you located there has me beat."

"Well, sir, we weren't exactly in the best of moods for detective work, in view of the livestock the place carries, but to me the whole case is simple. Shack with aerial on forbidden island adds up to secret radio transmitter and espionage - it's as easy as that."

"Very complicated to me, just the same, especially when one tries to tie it in with the lost anchor," he muses, more to himself than to us.

"What do you make of this anchor business, sir? On the face of it I'd say it seems such a load of rubbish . . . ."

"Quiet, lads . . ." our skipper warns as the Gondah shuffles along the companion-way, chanting in a woeful tone. "He's heard our voices and is hinting that we pipe down or else. Better douse that cigar, Honners, before he calls out the ship's fire-picket."

When the Gondah has departed Commander Bray whispers, "Cheer up, lads - in three days time we should reach our position in the vicinity of the legendary anchor. Peter can go down to have a sharp look-see, and this may help solve some of the mystery."

"How deep does it lie, sir?"

"According to the chart, some eight fathoms - thus it'll be a nice cushy plunge for a bit of practice, eh, Peter? Sandy bottom though, so you need to probe about somewhat. Obviously it's a tall order to locate anything as small as an anchor in mid-ocean, but I'm going to tell you something outside your range of comprehension - and mine. The Gondah will help. No, don't grin, I've seen stranger things than this out East. They say these temple charlies have a built-in metal-detection sense, rather like our own water-diviners. I've had it on good authority that they can locate a rupee at fifty paces."

I have been in Ramsam long enough not to blink an eyelid at the news about a Gondah-assisted search. Even Rana, despite her low I.Q., is so clairvoyant that it frightens you. For instance, up at Baada I lost my keys, so Rana retired to a dark room where she lit a candle and placed it in front of a white plate. For some time she stared at the flame, then told me I lost the keys near the tennis-courts and that they were lying in a kind of gully. I found them in the storm-drain by the tennis pavilion.

So I tell Commander Bray, "I don't care what the procedure is, as long as there's something doing at last. I'm fed up with sorting out the salvage gear of the Allied Nations like a commercial rep. doing up his samples."

At midnight the ship springs to life as five galleys light fires to cook five different feasts for all hands. Commander Bray and his officers do the rounds of the festive decks to tender greetings to the men and eat token offerings of delicacies. *En route,* we duck our heads to avoid the coloured lanterns hanging everywhere from the deckhead, so Commander Bray double-checks that the fire-picket is at the ready. Only the Gondah seems morose on this joyous occasion, as though he is still grieving about Honners having a cigar yesterday, but we salaam him as if nothing has happened.

"What about the ship's black-out, sir?" I inquire of our skipper, but he merely shrugs.

"Let the lads enjoy themselves while they can, Pook. I know we're a sitting duck but dawn is nigh and I don't reckon there's a sub within five hundred miles of us. We'll go aloft and check our bearings just the same."

For the next day or so Commander Bray and Honners check and re-check our position in an effort to pinpoint the lost anchor. By Monday noon they are confident that we are as near the spot as mathematics and diligence can accomplish.

"Not the easiest job in the world to locate a small object in mid-ocean," Commander Bray tells us for the hundredth time as though we keep insisting there's nothing to it. "Anyhow, I'll radio

N.H.Q. and put them in the picture, just to let them know we're on the ball. They have assured me we can do the job because we have the Gondah on board. They regard him as the finest aid to navigation obtainable - a cross between a spiritualist and Asdic gear. Commodore Gooji told me in all seriousness, let him loose with a palm-branch and he can detect a nail in fifty fathoms."

"The cock-eyed things we seem to accept in this Navy makes you wonder if we shall all be off our rockers before this trip is over," I cut in. "I'm supposed to be the crack diver of the Fleet, not a candidate for the Magic Circle."

"Watch it, Pook. Anyone who can walk barefooted over red-hot coals like the Gondahs do may consider metal-location quite a novicy chore. Could you do that for your party-piece, clevercuts?

"No, sir - I didn't get that far in the Diving Course at Pompey."

Our radio communication with N.H.Q. is something out of this world, especially when they send us a signal. The longest message we have received to date amounted to 4,500 words, covering twenty-seven sheets of signal-pad, which provided us with a condensed history of Ramsami theology. This was in reply to Commander Bray's terse signal, "Request permission to stand down for Toolu's Birthday." Since then our skipper has refused to send signals, preferring to speak direct to the innumerable officers at N.H.Q. who share in controlling our destiny. Even this unorthodox procedure has unforeseen snags because they are so excited at having the Fleet at sea that they want to talk with us day and night, asking such unprofessional questions as "Is it true that the horizon looks like a great circle right around the ship?"

Nowadays Commander Bray ignores any signal beginning, "Is it true that...?" Some messages contain details of the rice-crop up-country, while others require reports concerning the Belt of the Zodiac above us. Any gaps are filled by greetings from relatives to the crew, birthday messages, health inquiries, and lengthy recipes for the galley cooks.

What with the multi-lingual operators at both ends, many of the signals have to be checked back over the radio by voice-transmission before they make sense. The fact that we are supposed to be working under strict radio silence doesn't seem to bother anyone because the air is thick with short-wave transmission twenty-four hours a day.

Perhaps our strangest transmission is a request from N.H.Q. asking us to let them hear the roar of the mighty ocean as the *Soonong* ploughs south-eastwards through it. This performance is such a success that I am ordered to provide a fifteen minute commentary on the voyage for general broadcast by Radio Ramsam. I am compelled to narrate under the handicap of sitting beside the transmitter because we have no outside extension available from the Signal Distribution Office, so Honners helps me by poking his head out of the porthole and whispering back key words for me to enlarge upon, such as cloud, coconut, flying-fish, and so forth.

When he is overlong in spotting something of interest I improvise marine background by hissing into the microphone to indicate wind, tap a pencil to simulate the clatter of rigging, and murmur distant cries of approved nautical flavour such as "Avast there, me hearties!" and "By the mark, twain!"

Sea travel is usually so monotonous that in order to liven up the even tenor of our voyage I slant my commentary something like this: "... Astern the giant albatross - traditional omen of fortune to the sailor - still follows the gallant *Soonong* as she rides through the rolling main on her hazardous mission. (Honners has spotted a seagull aft.).... To starboard a ravenous twenty-foot blue shark waits impatiently for some poor sailor to be seized by the dread sea-fever and hurl himself over the side to his doom. (Honners thinks he has seen a herring.) . . . . On the port bow we sight wreckage from some ill-fated man-o-war and sadly we spare a thought for those unfortunate souls who perished in her. (Honners has seen the cook throw an empty beer-crate overboard.) . . . . Still to port we glimpse the massive shell of the Galapagos turtle, giant terrapin of the ocean, on which a man could lie down clear of the water. (Honners isn't sure, but thinks there may be a jelly-fish down by the Plimsoll line.) . . . . Near the horizon spouts the largest mammal known to man - the Odontoceti whale   . . . ."

N.H.Q. are greatly impressed by our performance, recording that there were tears in the eyes of Commander Gooji and Staff as they listened to my voice calmly narrating the perils of the deep as though I were in the next room.

But enough of reminiscence, because urgent business of war demands our attention. Monday forenoon the *Soonong* heaves to, and all hands peer excitedly over the starboard rail trying to spot the anchor we have come so far to find. They are pointing in all directions as the mind supplies what the eye cannot see, until Commander Bray is compelled to preserve the trim of the ship by ordering half of them to point over the port rail instead.

"All right, Pook, prepare for your first dive," the Commander orders in a voice half derisive. "We're in about six fathoms so there's nothing to worry about."

I remind him that men have drowned in as little as six inches before now, but nevertheless I am prepared to go down. Tension mounts as the Gondah waves his palm-leaf over the side and then gives me the go-ahead signal by dipping his shaven head towards me and turning his thumb downwards in case I am under the impression that diving involves my shinning up the mast.

This is the point of no return, as we say in the profession, so I sit down calmly and completely unafraid while my ratings force my body into the diving-dress with almost unnatural zest.

SEVEN

"Take your time, Pook. Have a good shufti round as far as your line will allow. Don't worry about using air - that's something we're not short of," Commander Bray instructs me, indicating the vault of heaven with his hand.

I am standing completely dressed in suit, corselet and boots, except for the helmet which my Petty Officer is holding in readiness. It is a landmark in the history of the Royal Ramsami Navy, being the first descent ever made by a member of that Service. My boyish curls blow carelessly from beneath the woollen cap and I smile debonairly as several of the crew photograph me with cameras supplied possibly by the Russian Embassy.

"When you've done with the publicity angle, Pook, come here and examine this," Commander Bray cuts in impatiently. I clump over to him in my massive 18-pound leaded boots to observe that he holds a dossier marked *Top Secret. Naval Intelligence. Anchors, Pijee Type.*

"Now, Pook, just in case you've never seen a hook before and don't know what to look for, scan this Top Secret photograph carefully."

"What, no wooden stock like the Victory had?" I complain. The hook is disappointingly commonplace. "It doesn't look anything like the one up in the sky."

Commander Bray gives me his smile of rank. "You don't

seem to know practically everything about the Service, do you, Pook?"

"As much as the next man, Commander. After all, I was in the Royal Marines - remember? *Per Mare, Per Terram* should ring a bell, even for you. Otherwise how could I be so smart ?

"What branch were you in then? The Royal Marine Artillery or the Light Infantry? By what I've seen of your seamanship I figured you were in the R.A.F."

Each day I find it more difficult to treat Bray like an officer and a gentleman, especially when he trots out this kind of lower-deck needle-talk. "At least I wasn't playing it safe in the R.N.R., if that's what you mean. Yacht clubs don't appeal to me."

"All right, Pook, no need to work yourself up so you won't be fit to dive. But notice how the shank of the anchor is fluted and made of metal. They tried wooden anchors for your benefit but they weren't really satisfactory, especially in water. Now, down you go, lad; best of luck and don't surface till you've got results, understand?"

The atmosphere is so tense that I am negligent enough to be involved in practically the only blemish on my career as a diver. It takes a big man to confess a fault, rather like the Chef of the Savoy admitting that once he burnt the toast, but what great artist has never made a mistake in his rise to the top of his craft? It happens this way. After checking the pump which two Shakalese ratings are cranking with practised rhythm, I signal my P.O. to screw the helmet down on my corselet and assist me to the ladder. Then I turn towards my Captain and, saluting with that precision I learned in the Royal Marines, suddenly stagger backwards as the deck rolls unexpectedly and fall off the ship upside-down.

Mercifully the breast-rope prevents my going too far down, so apart from a crack on my head and a damaged ego there is no real harm done. Only Commander Bray and myself are alarmed, because everybody else seems under the impression that this is standard entry drill, never having witnessed any other. I can hear my great boots scrape the ship's side as they turn me the right way up, and also the skipper's voice through the earpiece in my helmet.

"I fell over the side, sir," I explain simply. It is policy to make a clean breast of such a terrifying experience because these things are hard to evaluate in so many words to the layman.

"Well, when you come up, use the ladder, Pook - that's why we brought eight along. Don't put the fear of Hell into us by zooming back on board like a flying-fish. And in future you'll employ the diving-boat like I see it's laid down in Fleet Orders. You all right now?"

"All shipshape and Bristol fashion, Sir. Pay out plenty of line - I'm on the bottom already." I am indeed, grovelling in the muck to be honest, trying to overcome its suction and stand up without being buried alive. Whoever marked Sandy Bottom on the chart must have bombed longitudinally because it would seem I have been lowered down an oil-well.

Aided by shot-rope and distance-line I am supposed to begin a methodical search of the sea-bed spiral-fashion, thus enabling me to cover a wide area systematically without going over it twice. However, at the moment I am wondering how to start my circular route when only my helmet is above mud-level. Frankly, I am entombed in sludge, but my long experience offers two solutions. First, I can close the valve to inflate my suit and thus raise one's buoyancy. The snag here is that so much buoyancy may be required to overcome the suction of the mud that, once clear, I may shoot up into orbit, so to speak.

Prudence dictates the second course, which is to have my P.O. above heave me clear by means of the breast-rope without letting him know the predicament I am in down here. After the fiasco of falling off the ship it would not sound so hot if they find out on board that I am five feet below the sea-bed and still sinking in a kind of tropical Irish bog.

Wbile my P.O. heaves on the rope I make climbing motions to assist him, with the result that I squelch free like a corn being pulled from a foot. Keeping well away from the quagmire and adjusting my outlet-valve to maintain buoyancy I start the search in earnest, aided by the penetration of the sunlight which makes visibility surprisingly good. But try as I may, there appears to be nothing down here made by man.

Commander Bray phones to say he doesn't want me under longer than half-hour on an initial descent.

"Make it an hour, sir," I suggest, "then at least we'll know the whole area has been surveyed in our present position."

He agrees unwillingly, but just as well because it is not until the full extent of the distance-line is reached that I stumble across metal. Half buried in the ooze is a rusty old anchor. Excitedly I caress its crown and blades with trembling hands. What is more, there is that sticky feel about it reminiscent of Pijee oil ceremonial. From the ring hangs a length of the original cable still intact, and even in this light the delicate fluting along the shank is visible. It is undoubtedly the ancient bower-anchor we have sought so long.

Triumphantly phoning back the news I wait till Commander Bray sends down a one-inch lifting wire which I reeve through the ring and shackle back to its own part as neat as a spinster's hemstitch. Lastly I free the flukes from the mud by heaving it over on to its stock for easy lifting.

My part of the operation successfully completed, I signal that I am coming up and ascend slowly to witness the recovery from the deck of the *Soonong*.

"Well done, lad," Commander Bray congratulates me as he personally assists in the removal of my helmet. "You've accomplished the impossible in just over one hour flat. What a triumph for the old *Soonong.*"

"It's nothing really, sir - just luck coupled with skill, courage and observation," I protest modestly. "Though I don't see how it's going to win the war for us but at least it may solve the mystery of our assignment."

"Maybe the shank is hollow and contains a secret message?" Honners suggests melodramatically. I give this idea the contempt it deserves.

Meanwhile Commander Bray issues orders for the winch to take up the lifting wire through the derrick which has been swung over to starboard for this purpose. Very gently she goes, to avoid stress on the precious relic, but soon a great cheer swells from the crew as Pijee's anchor lifts clear of the water, dripping and weed-laden.

The Gondah stands by the rail, bowl of coconut-oil at the ready, salaaming to the swinging anchor as though it is his best friend being hanged.

"Looks as though Pijee's anchor has fouled our cable, sir," Honners observes to the skipper, drawing attention to the fact that running from the anchor is a cable which ends at the bows of the *Soonong.*

Commander Bray laughs this aside. "We'll soon clear that. The chief thing is that Pijee's anchor is safe and sound."

"With respect, sir, if that's our cable then where's our anchor? What I mean is, how come that Pijee's anchor is shackled to our hawse-holes?"

"Perhaps Pook got 'em mixed up under water."

"Then why are we drifting, sir?"

"Good thinking, Honners. Looks like we've had the bad luck to lose our own anchor. Never mind, Pook will locate it before sundown."

"But with great respect, sir, surely that's our anchor being winched inboard now. . . ."

"My oath! It's not humanly feasible but you're right, Honners. Where's Pook, the useless punk? Let me lay hands on that human crab - I've never seen a job crabbed up like this one. They send me the village idiot dressed as a diver and then wonder why I'm the laughing-stock of the Fleet. Well, when I'm through with him he'll be a city idiot instead . . . . "

Commander Bray is not a pleasant sight in anger so perhaps it is just as well that I am unavailable, being inside the recompression chamber. Not that I need recompressing but, sensing the connection between the anchor and our hawse-holes and realizing I have successfully salvaged the *Soonong's* anchor, I deem it wise to keep out of Bray's path till he calms down. Not that I attach much importance to the incident myself, mark you, because Columbus did a similar thing when he set out for India and got lumbered with America instead.

Apart from being on the carpet before the Commander I suffer the added humiliation of observing the *Soonong's* anchors being painted with alternating black and white stripes to avoid confusion in future. Then we search the area for the next three days but I fail to locate anything on the sea-bed except our own anchor, and as this is now easily identifiable I give it a wide berth.

Commander Bray signals N.H.Q. about the unsuccessful search but kindly makes no mention of the unfortunate mistake. The answering signal reads: "If at first you don't succeed, try, try again. Don't bother about this site any more but proceed to Position B and persevere with your usual tenacity of purpose. Who knows but this time success may be yours. A good start is half the battle, but Rome wasn't built in a day. We shall follow your progress with anxious hearts, so send us every scrap of news because all at N.H.Q. are enjoying your adventures immensely. You are doing a grand job and we trust that suceess will crown your endeavours. How we wish we were with you as you plough the main on your relentless probing of its secrets. Best wishes to all of you from all of us."

"Sounds more like a postcard from Blackpool than a Naval signal," I remark to Commander Bray, "but I suppose that's the price one pays for taking service under a bunch of fumbling amateurs. It would never have done in the Royal Marines."

"Well, Pook, at least we're at sea, which is more than you can say for the *Assang*. She was to be our support vessel but they couldn't get her out of harbour so she's back for a refit."

"But she's just had a refit."

"Perhaps the blessing ceremony was faulty - or maybe they forgot to paint her anchors black and white, eh?"

"Oh."

It is while we are searching the area around Position B that the notorious Cabada - the seasonal sou'easter - comes up and blows hard. In these parts one quickly finds that life is punctuated by the arrival of the Monsoon, the Peyana, the Cabada, and suchlike, but whatever insidious name they come under they all add up to the same thing - a dirty great wind which tries to blow you off the face of the earth.

On the second day of the Cabada Commander Bray decides that we can no longer maintain our position, let alone send me down again in such heavy weather. The met. forecast is so ominous that he signals N.H.Q. for orders and scowls puzzledly at the reply.

"On no account jeopardize the salvage equipment, so do whatever you think best. If it were me I would go home out of the storm, especially if it thunders like it does here at Jawanagar when Pijee and Toolu are quarrelling up in Tiboona. Can you find shelter anywhere? What about Nagar Kutupos Island on the chart? Such a lovely name; in Ramsami it means a school of sharks basking in the sun. If the crew go ashore and it thunders don't let them stand under the palm-trees. Our best wishes to you in your dire predicament. Rest assured that all at N.H.Q. are doing the needful by way of prayer and sacrifices."

Commander Bray throws the signal across to me with a snort. "Sometimes I wonder if they are just having me on, Peter."

"No, sir. By what we know of the Ramsamis I think they mean well - in all seriousness."

"Nevertheless that's the last time I signal for advice, seeing that Nagar Kutupos Island disappeared below the sea back in 1904. Our best bet is to abandon the search temporarily and try to steer clear of this sou'easter. If it comes to the worst we'll make for the east coast of India and shelter at Vizagapatam."

The *Soonong* weighs anchor and proceeds due west away from the path of the Cabada. As the gale lessens we gradually utilize the sails to speed our progress, but the wind freshens to such an extent that Commander Bray has them reefed lest we lose a mast.

The following morning Commander Bray is hard at work over his charts while I stare gloomily through the haze at the horizon. With binoculars I can see the lowlying coast of India and experience in these waters tells me it is not the best place to be in this kind of weather. Commander Bray has also seen it and he says, "Gentlemen, I don't fancy this at all. As you know, more ships are wrecked in this area than I care to remember. Common sense tells me to steam due east away from it but that entails taking the ship through the Cabada - not a healthy course for this old tub. Therefore I have decided to run for shelter at Vizagapatam."

"And that involves rounding Cape Madalla," I chip in cheerlessly. Cape Madalla, a lowlying sand promontory, is the local cemetery for unwary seamen as I found to my cost when I was attached to the Indian Navy - and one of the chief reasons why I am now in the Ramsami Navy.

"Exactly, Pook. The question is, can we beat round the headland without being driven ashore?"

"The answer is negative no. We can't - that's certain. Anything but that. Cape Madalla's beaches are littered with courts martial, loss of seniorities, Inquiries, severe reprimands, and half-pay Captains. I know every sandbank there - last year I couldn't keep off them even in fine weather. Sometimes it seemed that they actually came out to meet me."

"Cape Madalla is known as the Graveyard of Shipping," Honners adds miserably.

Commander Bray flares up at this. "Don't use that disgusting landlubber's cliché in my presence, Honners, understand? Despite the fact that I am surrounded by the cream of naval officers I intend to beat round Cape Madalla successfully."

"Then all I can say is we ought to steam at it full speed ahead so as to ground as far up the beach as possible. That'll save time and stop us getting wet when we tramp inland looking for a gharry to drive us down the road to Vizagapatam like we did last year."

"What did you say, Lieutenant Pook?"

"I said that your good seamanship and knowledge of the tides will pull us through safely, sir."

"That's better, lad. Good for you. Any questions, Honners?"

"No, sir - only that if *you* can't do it nobody can, as I shall testify at the Inquiry on your behalf."

"Pipe down, both of you. Pull together and we'll see this thing through in a blaze of glory if it's the last thing I do. Dismiss."

Honners and I hurry off to our stations in despondent mood. "Even Bray can't carry this off," I tell my friend, "not with a ship and crew like ours. One consolation, I know the district pretty well and there's some drinking pals of mine down at Vizag who'll put us up and lay on the odd party."

Honners screws up his face at this. "Wish I was as confident as Bray is, Peter. It's the wet bit in between I don't fancy. Frankly I'd rather be buried at sea than washed up on a beach. Excuse me while I check my life-jacket for moth."

It will long be argued in naval circles whether or not Commander Bray's brilliant seamanship could have navigated the *Soonong* safely clear of Cape Madalla if her engines had not packed up just as he was enlisting the aid of every trick in his repertoire. Unfortunately we shall never know because at the critical moment of the manoeuvre the air round the bridge was rent with China Coast language as a large red-faced officer pounded the rail with both fists, simultaneously reprimanding the heavens - and Pijee's Anchor in particular - in terms that the Gondah never forgave him for.

But even unbridled passion could not deprive Commander Bray of his nautical genius. Instead he took the unprecedented step of hoisting the giant jib and spinnaker in a fashion to delight the eye of old navy men so as to gather way on the stricken craft, although this meant that now we must be driven upon the shore by wind and tide even faster than we were drifting towards it.

"It's our only chance, Pook, to go in bows first," he roared at me, "or else we simply ground on the sandbanks beam-on - and have the rollers pound us to pieces in the process."

"That's what I told you to do in the first place, you doddering old ratbag," I replied, hoping the wind would drown my voice. I had been surveying these rollers for some time, massive spray-topped combers rolling in down the coast mile upon mile till they became invisible in the heat-haze round Cape Madalla. In fact so great was the distance that they appeared to move slowly, quite inaudible from the ship, like an old silent movie.

After much flapping, our giant jib ballooned out as the onshore wind tried to carry it away. Exploiting this and his helm, Commander Bray turned the *Soonong's* bows coastwards, then prepared to make the best terms he could with the inevitable. Although the white beaches were still but a hazy line in the distance, the rollers were already surging the vessel forward like a huge surfboard, until she quietly settled down on a sandbank. The Madalla coast had claimed yet another victim.

Our decks present a strange sight. The Gondah is frantically beating a gong up for'ard to summon the Ramsami ratings to attend his own emergency prayer session, while Commander Bray, Honners and myself are equally active to port and starboard trying to launch the cutters. Although we are all in the same predicament it would be an interesting study - if we had time for one - to examine how the two parties tackle the same problem.

Up for'ard the Gondah and the Ramsamis are invoking Pijee to save us by kneeling near the rail and scattering handfuls of rice on the sea. For his part, Commander Bray is attempting to gain the same objective by lowering the cutters. The Hindu and Moslem ratings helping us are under the impression that the boats are being lowered so that we may run the gauntlet of reaching the beach without being consumed by the rollers like tea-leaves caught in a drain. Consequently they find it difficult to understand why they are being ordered to stow kedge-anchors aboard each cutter.

"These are not Pijee anchors," they shrill in Hindustani, so why bother to save them? Who is worrying about stores at a time like this?"

Even more perplexing is Commander Bray's order to row, not for shore, but for the open sea. As he cannot leave the ship he sends Honners in one cutter while I take the other. We know the drill, always provided our craft can withstand the waves and keep nose to sea. Commander Bray figures that if two kedge-anchors are laid out to the stern of the *Soonong* he may be able to hold her fore-and-aft to the combers until the tide turns. In the secret recesses of his heart he even prays that eventually the combination of tide and anchors may pull us clear of the sandbank by means of skilful kedging.

I notice that Honners has attained the ultimate in marine courage by alternately giving orders to his crew and being seasick over the gunwhale. By now he is issuing very unprofessional commands such as, "Row like sin, you lazy rice-lovers, or else prepare to meet your Maker." Nevertheless he sticks doggedly to his task, gaining position and letting go his kedge-anchor several minutes before I am able to accomplish the same feat.

Returning to the *Soonong* is far more difficult than putting out. The swelling combers sweep us down on to the ship in terrifying fashion - so fast in fact that I see Honners' cutter dashed against the ship's side, staved in, and abandoned as all hands are heaved inboard by grabbing the netting Commander Bray has provided.

My own cutter, being well to port of Honners', is less fortunate. Strive as we may we are swept yards wide of the *Soonong* and onwards to the coast. Even as we race past I can see the Gondah leering at me and throwing over more rice on my behalf. Commander Bray hails me through the megaphone but all I can do is wave stupidly and struggle with the tiller in an effort to prevent our small craft capsizing. Nobody panics. My Moslem crew realize they are in trouble but they obey orders until the oars are swept from their hands.

Then the cutter is borne aloft by a massive comber, to be flung momentarily clear of the swell while we are engulfed below. I am turning over and over inside the belly of the wave until, when I can hold my breath no longer, some powerful force throws me with indescribable violence on to the beach. Strewn around the area in all directions are my bewildered crew, giving the beach the appearance that we have been jettisoned from a passing aeroplane. After making sure that no one is badly hurt, we form a wet crocodile for the long trek to the coast road I know so well.

My old friends of the Indian Navy at Vizagapatam show little surprise at my arrival on their premises. With casual but warm greetings of "Oh, so it's you again, Peter - how far up the coast have you left your ship this time?" they kindly pay off the gharry which has carried me along the dusty road from Cape Madalla, hand me a tot of whisky, and start kitting me up.

Directly I put them in the picture they phone the Port Captain and the Chief Salvage Officer to arrange for a tug to proceed northwards for the purpose of aiding the *Soonong,* provided she is not yet beyond human assistance.

But this is not the end of this extraordinary adventure. By now the *Soonong's* radio operator has recovered his wits sufficiently for communication to be established with Vizag, enabling us to speak direct with Commander Bray.

"Cancel the salvage tug, Peter," he roars jubilantly. "The kedge-anchors did the trick and we pulled ourself clear with the help of the tide and the engines, when they were repaired. Stay put in Vizag till I pick you up in the forenoon. I'm heading south this very moment."

"Wonderful news, Commander. Congratulations. Always thought you'd beat the Madalla shoals in the end."

"Don't give me the credit, lad; save it for the Gondah - he's claiming it anyhow. Says his rice offerings did the trick with Pijee and saved our bacon."

"What a load of bull!"

"Suit yourself - the main thing is that we're standing well off the coast under our own steam."

"How's Honners, Commander?"

"Pretty fit now we've fixed his wrist. He broke it when his

cutter hit the ship's side after the kedge-anchor was laid. Said to tell you he's looking forward to seeing you, and hopes soon to teach you how to handle a cutter when there's a bit of sea running."

"He could do, at that. See you by forenoon, sir."

"Hold hard, Peter. Wait until you hear this one. N.H.Q. in bedlam when they heard about everything. We're recalled immediately for an Inquiry, refit, 1,000-mile service, congratulations, blessing - the lot."

"But we've only been away three weeks!"

"There's a cable here for you, Peter, from Tina - she's missing you.

"Oh, that's different. Roll on Chattoo Dockyard, eh?"

"That's the spirit, lad."

EIGHT

Even in an epic of the seas such as this is, we have to spend a little time in port to get the tang of salt out of our pores and regain our landlegs once more by exercising them between taverns. So here we are back in Ramsam to be decorated for what Honners calls instant heroism, and standing in front of the Nawab on the dais of the Presence Chamber to receive our Ramsami Stars for going aground off Cape Madalla.

Commander Bray's reputation is deservedly tremendous after his gallant exploit. The Ramsami Intelligence refers to him as the Cheater of Death, comparable with Admiral Byng before he was court martialled and shot at Spithead, while Radio Ramsam names him as the staunch Ferryman of Pijee. Commander Bray doesn't relish being called a ferryman but he likes the glory nevertheless.

"Ah, Commander Bray, my bold navigator, congratulations on successfully retrieving your ship when you had run it aground by reversing it off the sandy shoals," the Nawab declares somewhat ambiguously. "The Gondah informs me you helped him save the vessel to the best of your ability after you had sailed headlong at the land for safety. You are a true son of Pijee indeed."

The son of Pijee scowls unappreciatively at the news as he backs off the dais with his decoration to make way for me. My two little broadcasts over Radio Ramsami have made my name a household word but they pale to insignificance after the exploit of the cutter which failed to return to the *Soonong*.

Nevertheless I feel certain that the blunder of salvaging our own anchor in error must sooner or later leak out via the crew, which prompts me to whisper in Honners' ear, "So far I'm getting a medal for failure. What do we get for success?"

"Nip up the steps and take your gong while it's going - it's pure gold," he advises.

There is some confusion during my presentation because the Nawab and I become slightly mixed up in the complex protocol pertaining to medal issue. I am saluting, salaaming, bowing, shaking hands and holding my palm out for the medal. Simultaneously the Nawab is saluting, salaaming, bowing, shaking hands and pinning the medal on my breast. Unfortunately we are doing these things out of time, which is most embarrassing to all concerned. On the second run-through I am holding my hand out for shaking but the Nawab is saluting; then he brings the medal forward for pinning on just as I am coming up for the double-handed Ramsami salaam. This knocks the Star up in the air, so I apologize with some confusion.

"Try keeping your arms to your side a minute, Lieutenant Pook, while I pin the Star to your breast," he tells me tersely. Then he fiddles about at eye-level, perforating my white uniform and outer skin with the clasp.

"Lieutenant Pook, you human crab, heartiest congratters, as you say back in your Island Home. The Gondah tells me you have introduced to our Navy the modern technique of painting the ship's anchors with black and white stripes. Most interesting. Now step back three paces, salute, salaam, shake hands and bow in that order, taking your time from me. Let us endeavour to synchronize our movements as the newsreel cameras are on us."

It is all very complicated but by following the Nawab's exquisite example I complete the routine and retire with my outsize gong to the assembled company.

Undoubtedly the hero of the hour is Honners, who has actually been wounded. A round of applause breaks out as he ascends the dais with his right wrist in a sling like a triangular tablecloth. Unabashed he salutes left-handed, bows, gives a one-armed salaam and shakes hands backwards - all with that polished ease which is the reward for hours of practice before a mirror.

In view of the size of the sling his Star has to be pinned to it for lack of chest space, causing more applause as the assembly voices its approval of this appropriate location of the medal. From my forward position I can hear what the Nawab is saying to Honners. "Ah, my small sea-going hero, how proud we are for what you have done to us. All Ramsam rings with shouts for the way you wrecked the cutter and broke your bones in the name of Duty."

"I would do it again, sir, to save my ship," Honners replies, none too pleased by the citation.

"Let us hope we shall be spared that, Lieutenant. May Pijee decree that next time you are up before me it won't be for wrecking anything but for doing something more constructive. May I add that what you have done so far you have done well - I am told it is a compound fracture, yes?"

Honners' features droop considerably as a result of this commendation, so he backs out of the royal presence much faster than he entered it, to join Commander Bray and me at the bar where we retail our conversations on the dais. Ramsam being a dry country, the bar displays a sign reading: "For European Officers and Friends Only."

"I didn't like the Nawab's tone, Peter," Commander Bray confides. "He knows every detail of the cruise, and my guess is he hears it all from the Gondah laddie. It's as bad as having a resident clairvoyant on the books - he can read your mind like a tax-inspector. Hold hard, here comes Commodore Gooji and Friends Only."

Commodore Gooji graciously accepts a glass of magga under protest, and then a strange conversation takes place between him and me. "Ah, Lieutenant Pook, here at the Europeans Only bar we can talk openly as man to man, no?" he smiles as an opening gambit. "I am hearing that you have been paying court to my daughter Kulima, yes?"

"I have?" This is news to me. The Commodore's family is so large and the female division so heavily clad in sarees and head-shawls that often one finds it difficult to locate Mrs. Gooji herself. Although full purdah is a thing of the past, the ladies still wear a kind of token head-dress and yasmak whereby nothing is visible except their beautiful big eyes. These the girls have learned to flash and roll as though wasps are stinging them lower down, with the result that usually I involuntarily wink my own eyes in return. Long ago Commodore Gooji sharply dismissed my suggestion that the ladies should be numbered on the back for easy identification like footballers.

"'Even a fool can see there is something going on between you and my lovely Kulima, Peter."

"You can, sir?

"Ah, so we are shy, are we, Peter?" the Commodore persists archly, digging me in the ribs with his elbow.

"Not shy - just surprised," I laugh back, returning the shove to Commodore Gooji's cummerbund.

"So, Peter my boy, you are bashful at the prospect of becoming my son-in-law perhaps, eh? Think what an advantage that would be to your naval career."

This alarms me because although I can see his point, I can also perceive the disadvantage of not becoming his son-in-law once given the offer. "Who told you of this affair, sir?" I inquire, stalling for time. A situation is always difficult when you don't know the party concerned.

"Dear Kulima herself hinted at it to Mama, though of course it was obvious to us all." I trust it isn't obvious to my girl-friend Tina but say nothing. "In fact my wife hopes you will come over and join the ladies right now for a few minutes, eh, Peter? Let us tear ourselves away from the Europeans Only bar, shall we?"

Commodore Gooji leads me across the floor to his family who, as usual on these occasions, are lined up in dejected ranks staring silently into space. I scan the ladies to see if I can spot Kulima, but everybody seems to possess the same beautiful eyes, with the mole-like caste-mark dead centre between them. I bow into the two-handed salaam, which is given by bringing one's finger-tips together as though demonstrating the pitch of a roof to a shortsighted builder. The ladies bow and giggle delightedly.

"Please don't be offended, Peter," Commodore Gooji explains quietly, "your salaam was perfect - they are only laughing at your hair. Allow me to introduce my wife."

He turns to the widest lady and recites the introduction formula, whereupon Mrs. Gooji extends her hand so high that I have no option but to kiss it in mid-air.

"Ah, Pook Sahib, do not waste kisses on an old lady - - better bestow them on one who deserves them," she chaffs frankly. "Run along and greet your little Kulima who awaits you so impatiently."

To be on the safe side I salaam all seven daughters in turn, closely observing each pair of eyes for a hint of identification.

Secretly I hope Kulima is number five in the line because this girl flutters eyelashes like moth's wings and oscillates her eyebrows as though they are elastic-bands. Apart from that, nobody offers me a clue, so turning aside to the Commodore I whisper, "Sorry to appear dull today, sir, but which of your hooded lovelies is Kulima?"

"You mean you have forgotten so soon, Peter?"

"Well, be fair; there's not a lot to remember, is there? Only two eyes and a caste-mark."

Commodore Gooji leads me to number five, who stares at my feet and giggles. Her father says roguishly, "Run along, the pair of you, and pour out your hearts to one another. Be off, you naughty sweethearts!"

Diplomatically under the circumstances I grope for Kulima's hand but it is unavailable beneath the folds of her saree, so automatically I lead the way to the bar - though how she will drink with a yasmak and no hands is beyond my comprehension. Kulima squeals protestingly at the sight of the bar, indicating that convention demands we sit together with her family.

Consequently we return to seats among her sisters and park there in silence. Occasionally the girls steal a glance at me, giggle, and stare at the floor. Obviously the party is not going too well. I smoke a cigarette but everyone coughs so alarmingly that I stub it out. Suddenly inspiration prompts me to display my medal for their inspection but as they apparently have no hands I am obliged to hawk it round the group as though trying to sell it. The girls hiss pleasure noises through their teeth and giggle without making any comment.

"This is the medal the Nawab gave me." I explain feebly, indicating his features on its face. "It is the Ramsami Star.

It is made of gold. This is the ribbon it hangs from. Red, yellow, and green are the colours on the ribbon - see?"

Obviously I am running out of conversation and running into Ramsami phrase-book exercises. It occurs to me that I won the medal for far less than what I am doing at the moment. Also I wonder how on earth Commodore Gooji learned from his taciturn daughter that she loves me. I decide he must be psychic.

Eventually I make my exit from seven pairs of eyes on the

pretence that Commander Bray is signalling me across the chamber. This ruse enables me to join him at the bar but on the way over a queer thing happens. As one of Commodore Gooji's Aides passes me he calls out, "Congratulations, Lieutenant Pook - I hope you will both be very happy together." Before I can question him he disappears.

"Oh, watch it, Peter," Commander Bray warns when I have put him in the picture. "This sounds dangerously like Omorani to me."

"And who is Omorani when she's in port?" Everybody round here seems to live in a different world to mine.

"Omorani roughly translates into shotgun wedding, Peter. A marriage is proposed by the Establishment and all hands accept it as an accomplished fact - including the . bridegroom. In other words you are shoved into it by long-term auto-suggestion."

"But why pick on Kulima and me for heaven's sake?"

"Many reasons, Peter. For one thing, Gooji has seven daughters to launch. Also it's a feather in his cap if the girl weds a European - even of your stamp. Another point -maybe people don't like you going around with Tina."

"Why ever not?"

"Well, she's probably a spy. Then again, she's not of the blood - she's chi-chi - half-caste. Finally, I hear strong rumours that you told Mrs. Smith up at Baada that you loved her daughter, Powerful Peg. Whatever it is, you can bet your dowry the Nawab is behind it."

I laugh coldly. "Listen, Commander. I told everybody in Baada I loved them - it was the climate up there. Secondly, I don't even know Kulima, let alone marry her. Lastly, I like Tina and that's that. I'm for diving, not for marrying."

"Not so fast, Peter. This is Ramsam, not Fulham. Here there are wheels within wheels. Rumour has it that the name of Pook, the human crab, is linked with that of the Nawabani herself."

"Don't be ridiculous, Commander. Apart from one Robbers at the Pijee Palais we've hardly met."

"Nevertheless Mrs. Smith told me the Nawabani asked you to dance with her - then you embraced closely and indulged in a lot of familiar harem-type chat."

"So what?"

"Peter, out here junior officers just don't dance with the Nawab's wife - it's not done."

"Well, I'm no snob - I'll have a go with anyone."

"It's the other way round, Peter. The top crust don't want to have a go with you - unless you want to end up as court gigolo or something."

"Oh."

This heavy conversation is mercifully interrupted by Tina, who isn't quite so friendly nowadays on account of my name being linked with everybody I know and some I don't. "I'll have a gin-and-it, Peter - then, if you can spare the time for an old flame, we might exchange pleasantries," she purrs off-handedly.

Smiling esoterically I order the drink. Experience has taught me that a reputation is a great booster for one's popularity, while instinct tells me that the best way of keeping Tina is to play hard to get. Hard, but not impossible. Furthermore, women thrive on intrigue, so that in the past, when short of it, I have found it good tactics to cook some up. Some people say this policy is why I am still single.

"Oo-la, lovely!" Tina murmurs, sipping her drink and looking at me with the tops of her eyes. "So, darling, how are we? Or should I say how's your love life, eh? Difficult these days to meet anyone who isn't practically engaged to you."

"You know how it is, Tina. Things can be tiresome when girls find one so attractive. All my life I've tried to prevent myself becoming a toy of *l'amour.*"

Sensing that Tina has gone all moody and is preparing some verbal body-blows I relax in order to meet her on her own ground. Consequently I smile mockingly, shrugging my shoulders to indicate that I am British if nothing and do not discuss affairs of the heart in public.

"What a lovely shiny medal, Peter," she says, absentmindedly clinking her glass against my decoration. "It makes one wonder what you would have received if you had located Pijee's anchor instead of the *Soonong's.*"

Glancing hurriedly to ensure that Commander Bray is out of earshot I gulp down a full magga glass, but Tina perceives she has confused me by a flank attack.

"Don't fret, Peter - nobody shall know except the two of us and the fish. Anyway why talk shop when the party is so gay? Let me give you a toast: Better luck next time."

Tina is laughing at me, so I join in sportingly as though I enjoy it. "You've never looked lovelier than tonight, darling," I tell her intensely.

"That's better, honey - that's my old Peter. Kiss me to show you mean it."

"What, here! In front of all my women?"

"Of course. What choice have you? A full embrace please. You've never been shy before."

Blackmail comes in assorted packages, so I lean over and peck her cheek quickly, like a snake striking, then retire modestly. Whereupon Tina puts both arms round my neck and hangs on blissfully while the assembled company fix me with that stare usually reserved for carrion. Although disciplined almost to the point of celibacy I am human enough to let her have it right on the mouth with a kiss of such power that her shoulder-straps slip down.

Understandably I am so engrossed that I hardly notice the flash-bulb go off as the bored cameraman of the Ramsami Intelligence at last finds an item of human interest for his editor. I feel Commander Bray digging me in the ribs and hissing, "Belay there, Pook. You should know better than behave like that before the top Ramsami brass . . . er . . . er . . . ."

Commander Bray so seldom stutters that I put Tina down to give him a piece of my mind. For one thing I abhor his habit of addressing me as though I am jolly Jack Tar of the Trafalgar wall-prints series, with his *belay there* and *reef your topgallant* every time I open my mouth in public. However, he is escorting no less a person than the Nawabani herself, so we all bow into the two-handed salaam which provides me with a welcome lull for wit-gathering. Observing that the Nawabani and Tina are indulging in some sharp ocular signals I decide to try out my Ramsami dialect as a peace-feeler.

This is a sure-fire party livener. I give the local equivalent for "Do you come here often?" and everybody laughs at the sound of an Englishman talking in a foreign tongue.

"Ah, Pook Sahib, so you are mastering our difficult language, eh?" the Nawabani smiles charmingly.

"I struggle on, ma'am, undeterred."

"How thoughtful of you - and how necessary in your present complicated position. Our dear Kulima has almost no English."

"And precious little Ramsami either, ma'am."

"Oh, fie on you, Pook Sahib! Soon you will be knowing well the language of love, then you will find Kulima is quite a little chatterbox. Perhaps at the moment she is a tiny bit jealous - we of Ramsam are not accustomed to kissing in public."

"Naturally, ma'am. There is a proper time and place for everything."

"Ah, Pook Sahib, so you are wanting to be alone with her, of course. Commodore Gooji shall arrange for you to take her to the bioscope to see a Ramsami film, then you two sweethearts will be alone and completely in the dark together."

"I couldn't be more in the dark than I am at the moment, m'am," I complain truthfully.

It is surprising how quickly such matters can be arranged in the East when they put their minds to it and stop rambling on about Eternity. Commodore Gooji and his Aides programme a tryst for Kulima and me the following evening by booking the entire balcony of the little Bijou Bioscope in order that we may see a double-feature bill suitable to our state. It seems we are to witness *Bride of Frankenstein,* followed by the greatest saga ever to be produced in the Orient entitled *What Happened To Kadu When He Met Volani During The Feast Of Pijee.*

In order to preserve the proprieties our party arrives at the Bijou in eight gharries, discreetly segregated according to sex. There are five gharries for the gentlemen, three for the ladies. I am in the second gharry, squeezed in between Commodore Gooji and Aides wearing full dress as though I am under close arrest. Altogether our parties number forty-six chaperones. The manager personally greets us in the foyer. Here the introductions are so protracted that a small sweating man in a dhoti appears out of a box to tell the manager something about his projector being red-hot.

Up in the balcony the gentlemen sit to the left, the ladies to the right. I am placed in the middle of the row as sole contact between male and female groups, with the Commodore on one side and an empty seat on the other. Eventually a veiled lady in a dupa saree glides along the aisle to this seat as though she is on castors. "Do you come here often?" I inquire, employing my standard conversational gambit in Ramsami. The lady shakes her head in vigorous denial.

"Don't you like movies then, ma'am?"

She nods her head and registers supreme bliss with her eyes. This passion for the cinema probably explains why she is trembling. Having run out of mime and vocabulary I turn to Commodore Gooji. "Where's Kulima then, Commodore?" I ask. Surely I don't have to woo the lass by proxy.

"Sitting on the other side of you, Peter - as you wished it to be. Let us hope her prattling little tongue does not interrupt the programme for us, so much is she loving you and the bioscope."

"Oh!"

"This is her very first visit to the bioscope, thus she may appear somewhat nervous."

"She seems to be terrified. I put it down to *The Bride of Frankenstein.*"

"Perhaps it is your presence - so close, eh, Peter?" the Commodore chuckles roguishly. "How do you like my beautiful daughter? She has a formidable dowry."

"She has lovely eyes too," I reply, filing the dowry item in my memory. "Perhaps one day you will permit me to see her nose. To be frank, sir, it is difficult to court a young lady when there's so little point of contact. Can't she get her hands outside the saree? She sits there like she's handcuffed."

"Ah, Peter, we must be patient, mustn't we? I never saw my wife's face until we were engaged - it was hard to bear, believe me, but such is our custom."

"Especially when you've got to live with it for the rest of your life, sir. You certainly lost out there. When did you first see her hands then? - on your honeymoon?"

"Shush, Peter - here is coming the Anthem."

When we rise for the Anthem I whisper to Kulima, "Stand up, dear - it's the Anthem," but her father tells me she is already standing up. I have not noticed before how short she is, causing me to wonder why Commodore Gooji did not match her with Honners. The Nawab's handsome face leers at us from the screen as his palace shakes to the thunder of the Royal Salute being fired in the background, until an enormous thumb-shadow appears and whips him off, to be replaced by birth-control ads.

I offer Kulima some cachou-nuts which she declines. Actually this is pure experiment on my part to see if there is any channel of communication through to her lips. Then we settle back to watch *What Happened To Kadu When He Met Volani During The Feast Of Pijee*. It is not easy to discover Kadu's fate because the dialogue is in Ramsami. Subtitles flash on in Urdu at the bottom of the screen, while at the top appear the same captions in Burmese. Moreover, my attention is drawn to a small side screen which carries the dialogue in Tamil, Arabic, and English.

I try following the picture on the big screen and the English subtitles on the side screen until a bout of double vision grips me. Then I lose the thread of the complicated plot entirely, so I relax, grateful to shut my eyes and blot out the flashing subtitles completely. Kulima is not only enthralled by the story but also reading all the subtitles. I can tell this because her head is jerking about like a hen in a corn-chandlers. "You must be multilingual, dear," I whisper to relieve the monotony.

But half-way through the film the dialogue is drowned entirely by a roaring noise like a storm at sea. This cannot be connected with the plot because whatever happens to Kadu inevitably inspires him to break out into a national dance like knee-football in slow-motion.

"It's a hailstorm on the tin roof of the bioscope," the Commodore explains to me. "You'll have to follow the dialogue on the side screen until it subsides. At the moment Kadu is saying he loves Volani so dearly that he is going to dance in front of the village elders to prove it."

"What was he dancing for just now then?"

"Oh, he was so unhappy because Volani refused to dance with him at the Festival of Pijee. She preferred the dancing of Tooba, Kadu's rival. You see, if the Gondahs approve of his dancing they will let him dance before Volani's house later on in the dance of the swains."

"Is he a professional dancer then?"

"Oh, no, Peter. Can't you read? He's a cobbler."

So ends yet another of those strange conversations I hold every day in Ramsam which are gradually sapping my desire to speak to anybody. But it is during the long interval that the shock comes.

Commodore Gooji inquires how I have enjoyed the programme so far. "Wonderful," I lie, "wouldn't have missed it for worlds."

"Poor, poor Kadu, eh?"

"Properly gone for a burton, sir." Actually I couldn't care less so long as he doesn't revive after the interval.

"All his dancing didn't win Volani, eh, Peter?"

"Probably had a heart attack. He was on the hoof nearly two hours. No wonder Volani preferred Tooba - at least she could pin him down for a kiss or two between dances."

Commodore Gooji looks at me slyly. "Peter, why are you not asking Kulima how she is liking the picture?"

"Because Kulima is not answering anything I say. Maybe I should get up and jig to encourage her." Between ourselves I am speculating if she is a deaf mute.

"Try, Peter."

I smile at her and say, "How are you liking the interminable film, Kulima dear?" The girl rolls her eyeballs and waves her head from side to side in a frenzy of approbation.

"Ah, the dear sweetmeat is overwhelmed by so much pleasure," Commodore Gooji comments. "She is little used to such company or such entertainments."

"She's led a very sheltered life I guess?"

"But of course. As befits a woman of Ramsam her reputation has been guarded with jealousy - awaiting the man of her choice. Perhaps he has come at last, eh?"

"Did she actually say so, or did she write you a note?

"Ah, Peter, I should not tell you these things, but at night she pours out her heart to Mama and me about you. It is a torrent of passion, believe me. Often we are having to check her in full stream to get a word in edgewise."

"Then she sees me and dries up?"

"Exactly. Only last week was her birthday, and she nearly drove us mad with her prattle about inviting you for the party. Day and night her little tongue was wagging about her Pook Sahib, the human crab."

"You should buy a dictaphone and record it. I could at least play it back when we're alone together - and who knows but when we're engaged she'd even mime to it" I stop short and kick myself for mentioning an engagement. I look sideways at the Commodore to see if he has noticed my slip of the tongue but he too is looking sideways at me and wearing his father-in-law smile. I try to fight my way clear by throwing in carelessly "But of course she's too young yet for anything like that."

The Commodore is merciless. "Ah, Peter my boy, you have the full consent of your mother and me - and the loving welcome of your brothers and sisters you have come to know so well. In fact your whole family takes you to its bosom this moment - from now on you are a complete and utter Gooji. No, my son, don't try to thank me, just let me set you mind at rest lest you think you are too old for your wife. She is in the full bloom of womanhood."

"How old is that then?" I ask, trying to stall for time."

"The correct marriageable age, Peter, as you can see."
"Yes, I know - but how old in years?"
"Twelve."

Fortunately the lights dim at this moment, allowing me to shrink into my seat and collect my wits as another conversation ends with shattering impact. I sit there sweating, and wonder if I can stand much more of the esoteric life in Ramsam - but at least one thing is resolved in my mind. Even if it means resigning my commission and losing a fortune in dowry I am not going to be bulldozed into walking up the aisle with an infant.

However, Fate has something even worse in store for me of such a nature that sensitive readers will do well to skip the next chapter and read on with a high-minded sense of disappointment. I always like to warn folks when a purple passage is coming so that they may put the book out of reach of adults in the family.

NINE

They say it never rains but it pours, and this is certainly true with one's love affairs - but it never poured harder than it does on Commander Bray's birthday. Of late it is noticeable how Rana has been eyeing me with her dark flashers as though I have come into money. Not that she neglects Commander Bray, but his unpredictable moods are heavy on all of us especially when he is on the booze.

Although virtually woman-proof and strictly a career man I don't discourage Rana's attentions. At the back of my mind is that long period of senility in the distant future when women will look upon me as a crumbling sugar-daddy warming his old bones in the Riviera sun, so I believe in gathering one's rosebuds before the blight sets in. Consequently I am not surprised when she asks me to take her out - merely disappointed she has waited so long.

"I want you to go with me down to the bad part of the town, Peter," she announces in that soft voice women employ when they are utilizing their sex to get the earth.

"You mean there's a worse part than this end?" I exclaim. Shaggapore must deteriorate sharply to the east.

"Oh, everybody is very wicked there. That is why I want you to escort me, please, Peter."

"Why can't we be wicked up this end? Are you afraid someone might catch us?"

Rana laughs mysteriously. "I am wanting to surprise Commander Bray you see, Peter."

"What will he be up to in the eastern quarter then?"

"Ah, he will not be there - that is how we shall surprise him."

"Have it your own way, dear; it's too hot to argue." Lately I agree with everybody, on the grounds that when it comes to logic I am fast becoming the local village idiot around here.

"You see, Peter, the Commander is reading *Sailing Alone Around the World* to me until we are both knowing it by heart. Sometimes he is mentioning another book he would like to read me, called *Submarines- A World Without Women* by Unterseeboot Kapitan Starkheim of the German Grand Fleet, but it is out of print. Maybe we could find this book in the second-hand bazaars down town."

"If you don't mind my mentioning it, dear, he doesn't exactly sound the romantic type judging by his reading-list. Why not go the whole hog and buy him *Jack the Ripper?*"

"Oh, no, Peter, he is particularly anxious to read me this book *Submarines - A World Without Women* - he told me so. Thus I am wishing to present it to him on his thirty-ninth birthday."

"Then you're too late - he celebrated that years ago." Bray has been thirty-nine so long that he must have a phobia about the forties and intends to shamble straight into the fifties. Rana ignores the comment with "Will you please help me, Peter? "

"Everything has its price, dear," I remind her.

We choose Saturday evening for our shopping expedition because this is late closing night down in the bazaars where they keep open till 4 a.m. Sunday morning. Jogging along eastwards in a gharry is quite pleasant with a girl like Rana because it is too warm for a monologue and we both find it interesting to survey the dirty buildings and quaint folk *en route*. For a more complete description of an Eastern bazaar area such as this one, see any television travelogue.

The gharry halts at the boutique of one Mr. Matalia, who is dressed all in white as though he is also a surgeon on the side. We observe that he has remarkably large toes and wears a kind of toilet-roll hat on his head, presumably to indicate his trade of bookseller. We enter his boutique as best we can through the piles of dusty volumes which appear to be supporting the ceiling. Outside on the pavement are more racks of books in such profusion that one wonders what he does with them when he closes. Certainly they cannot be brought inside because we are squeezed into a kind of catacomb built entirely of literature.

"What can I do for the Sahib and Memsahib, please?" Mr. Matalia inquires, bowing as low as his stock will permit.

"We are looking for a book called *Submarines - A World Without Women* by Unterseeboot Kapitan Starkheim, and thought you might have a copy handy," I tell him. By the look of the shop there can hardly be any work he hasn't got handy.

"Ah, yes, Sahib, I understand," he replies, leering at me knowingly. "A most excellent book indeed by one of Germany's foremost espionage agents. It is here of course, so kindly wait while I put my hand on it."

This is good news but I can tell by the vague way he rolls his eyes over the stock that it may take some time for his hand to alight on this particular volume. Very soon the three of us are scanning the piles in the hope of locating the title, without success.

"Haven't you any kind of index here?" I ask him. Dewey didn't have this type of establishment in mind when he invented his classification system.

"Oh, yes, Sahib," he replies, waving his arms as if to indicate that under his system one does not enter a Ramsami bookshop for a specific title but accepts what Fate may offer, "we keep everything in the order of its arrival on the premises."

Our search is interrupted by the entry of a large lady who is introduced to us as Madam Matalia. She shakes my hand warmly, apologizes for keeping me waiting, and regards Rana with some surprise.

"Who is this girl?" she demands, raising her pencilled eyebrows and blinking her violet eyelids puzzledly.

"This is Rana, my friend and book-lover," I explain.

"Oh, indeed. How unusual. So, you naughty boy, as you say in England you are bringing coals to Newcastle, eh? Does she need a job?"

"No, thanks. She's well looked after."

"Good. Then she must wait in the hall, though I never heard of such a peculiar arrangement. It is enough to make me the laughing-stock of the district. Follow me please, Pook Sahib and book-lover - if you ever heard of such a thing."

"Can you find *Submarines - A World Without Women* by Unterseeboot Kapitan Starkheim for me, Madam Matalia?" Even as I say the phrase it sounds like a password.

Madam Matalia laughs uproariously. "But of course, dear boy - there are many German spy books here. This way please. How strange are the ways of the British - a book-lover indeed! How very droll. Always I am learning something new."

The lady leads us through the rear of the shop where we cross a yard and walk down an alley to a high wall which is breached by a huge double wrought-iron gate. This gate is swung back for our entry by an outsize chokidar wearing semi-military uniform. I glance at Rana but she is silent. This trip is undoubtedly linked to espionage, though it is impossible to guess whether Rana is implicated or not. Thinking back quickly it occurs to me that she probably is because she arranged the whole affair in the first place - all on a pretty thin pretext.

To my shrewd mind the set-up is patently a trap, but on the

other hand if I see it through it may provide me with an opportunity to get on the inside and split the espionage racket wide open. Moreover I can hardly be in mortal danger here in the heart of Shaggapore, especially as my absence would soon be noticed back at base, albeit with glee. As the big iron gates clang behind us I feel a tremor of excitement accompanied by a pleasing mental flash of the Nawab handing me the Ramsami Cross for counter-espionage activities beyond the call of duty.

If the boutique was dingy then this house is a palace. I take in the sumptuous hall at a glance but my fears of espionage are confirmed because although it appears to hold many art treasures there is not a book to be seen. I remark upon this to Madam Matalia who seems amused. "Our library is over there, Sahib," she smiles, pointing to a double-doored entry at the rear of the hall, "but I am afraid your pretty book-lover cannot come further than here. Perhaps she will be so kind as to take a seat by the fountain."

I check on the marble fountain and am entranced by the fish in its waters. "Fancy having a real fountain and pool in your hall, Rana. Have you seen it before?" I ask her craftily.

"No, Peter, of course not. Never in my life have I been in this quarter of the town and I am not in love with it. Please go for the book and return as soon as possible. I am not liking this oily woman or the way she leers at you."

By the worried tone of her voice I wonder if maybe this is not her own organization after all. If so, I am the last person to get her in a jam but it is too late now for pulling out. Nevertheless I wish I were armed, just to be on the safe side. Madam Matalia claps her beringed hands with surprising force, whereupon the doors open and I walk through with that confident strut I always employ when nervous. I can easily deal with the odd wog but a sten-gun aft is a different matter.

This room is the biggest and most luxurious library I ever saw, but it seems that to make it even more spacious they have taken all the books away. Madam Matalia motions me to a divan, whereupon I sit bemused by the oriental surroundings and a murmur of Ramsami zithers off-stage. By my side is a portable cocktail-cabinet decorated with phallic emblems."

"I don't want to rush you, Madam Matalia, but we don't have all night to spare," I tell her casually, as though Boots Library is just like this at home. "Could you bring me *Submarines - A World Without Women* as soon as possible so we can be on our way?"

Madam Matalia beams happily. "What a pleasure it is to have the patronage of a British officer - so calm, so discreetly indirect. How different to some of our more emotional clientele from nearer home - they destroy all the sophistication of life with their coarse behaviour and impatient demands. Just help yourself to a peg of magga while I fetch the little book-lover you desire."

Just as she is about to disappear through the curtains at the far end of the room she turns to remark, "Oh, how discourteous of me to forget - if you find it too warm in here please take your clothes off."

This is the queerest literary set-up in my experience - so improbable that the very outlandish atmosphere of it holds me intrigued. Nevertheless I help myself to the magga tray and borrow some of the Turkish cigarettes alongside. If this is the local custom for bibliophiles I may as well take advantage of it. One thing is certain - it never happened to me back in London.

I am so busy at the bar that at first I don't hear Madam Matalia returning. By her side slinks the silliest gimmick you ever saw - a girl wearing a little transparent yasmak to cover the lower half of her face. A transparent yasmak seems to defeat its own ends, but what is even more unorthodox about the girl's dress is that she isn't wearing any.

"She must sure be hot," I observe mundanely, hoping the door between Rana and me is securely locked. Automatically I swig the rest of the magga, forgetting my old rule that the undrinkable may lead to the unthinkable.

"Ah, Pook Sahib, this is Kapiti, my extra-special number one girl," Madam Matalia explains. "Just look at her marvellous teeth."

Kapiti modestly raises her yasmak so I may examine the least prominent feature about her. Each front tooth has been filled with a diamond, so that when she smiles they flash disconcertingly. It occurs to me that to date we are not getting very far either in the field of espionage or the world of books but there are distinct possibilities in other directions.

"What lovely teeth you have, dear," I praise her dutifully. They must be good because they are the only things she keeps covered up.

"Kapiti is a very busy girl, Sahib, but she has been waiting tonight especially for you," Madam Matalia discloses.

Characteristically I come straight to the point. "All right, Madam Matalia, what does she want to know?" Under the circumstances I figure it would be better to come to terms early than be vamped into it by Kapiti while Rana frets outside clock-watching. When all is said and done, I am not made of balsa.

"Kapiti wants to know if you want to know her," Madam Matalia explains, apparently under the impression I am a snob. For my part I can't see much point in being formal when one of the parties is in the nude. However I always respect local customs, so I shake Kapiti by the hand and inquire in Ramsami if she comes here often. Receiving no answer I remark upon the weather, adding lamely, "Are you the librarian, Kapiti?"

The girl looks puzzled, as though she has never read a book in her life. "This naughty English Sahib has brought his wife with him - she is waiting in the hall," Madam Matalia explains, "but they say everything has a first time."

The mention of Rana brings me back to earth with a jerk. "I don't want to appear rude, Madam, but please let me have the book quickly - I can't stay here all night."

"You are wanting to sign in for short time only, eh,?"

"No, I want to buy it for keeps and take it home"

"That is what they all say, Pook Sahib, but Kapiti is my number one girl and not for sale."

We seem to be talking at cross purposes, but Madam Matalia speaks briefly to Kapiti in Ramsami. I catch the word *nautch*, whereupon the girl raises both hands above her head, clicks her fingers, sways her hips, and begins that monotonous form of torso-rotation known in Ramsam as dancing. "I will leave you two alone together now, Sahib. Kapiti is performing for you the dance of love," Madam Matalia explains archly. "Just watch the emerald on her navel and soon you will be forgetting all your troubles."

Some hidden disc-jockey turns up the zither music while Kapiti's bare hips and taut thighs oscillate in time with it like a ship's piston. My eyes are fascinated by the way she retains the emerald amidships without visible means of support. Involuntarily I myself begin to hula as though polishing a window with my bottom, whereupon Kapiti smiles and says "Clever, clever! Let us dance together, Sahib."

Pausing only to synchronize our hula movements, the beefy wench rams me with her breasts and fastens her arms round my neck. The dance of love may be erotic in the extreme but a glance in the wall-mirrors lets me know that it certainly isn't dignified. In fact, if Madam Matalia is filming it with a hidden camera then I am a dead duck. One can just imagine the Nawab asking at the Inquiry, "And what are you doing in this scene, Pook? Struggling with an octopus in forty fathoms?"

It is while I am in this compromising situation that Rana bursts through the door, followed by a very distraught Madam Matalia.

"Quickly, Peter, run for your life!" she cries optimistically, apparently beyond taking in my novel position.

"It is the cursed police - they are raiding us again," Madam Matalia adds at a more practical level. One glance over Kapiti's shoulder shows me the futility of running on any pretext because five Ramsami sepoys carrying well-dented lathees fan out across the library floor, followed by their officer, a full-blown Jemadar.

"Ah, a good night's work!" he exclaims with relish. "A European naval officer wearing his uniform. Surely you must be knowing, Sahib, that this kind of practice is illegal in our country, the same as drinking and revolting." His tone warns me he has come to arrest rather than rescue me. Taking out a notebook as if he is conning me for a parking offence he says, "Name and address, please, Sahib, and what is your story for being here?"

"I came here to buy a book," I tell him frankly.

"Yes, yes, that is what they all say," he chuckles. "Can you not do better than that, Sahib. Visiting a sick relation perhaps? Or dancing lessons? Lost your way in a London fog?"

"I'm telling you I came merely to buy a book - got it? Then Madam Matalia here started to con me with the help of this girl - obviously an espionage decoy."

"Good, good. Keep talking, Sahib. This is a new one and will liven up the Inquiry, especially as you brought your wife with you. All original material. Drop the book angle please - we are having this one till we are tired of hearing."

"I am not this man's wife," Rana cuts in emphatically.

"Good, good. Most interesting. You are just good friends, eh? Sahib brings his mistress to house of ill-fame as interpreter, eh? Excellent. Who are you please?"

"Ask Commander Bray; he will vouch for me," Rana replies spiritedly. "Commander Bray would not humiliate me in this disgraceful fashion - he is a gentleman."

"Commander Bray, eh?" chuckles the Jemadar, jotting every item in his notebook. "He is your husband, yes?"

"No, he's not."

"Hoo, hoo - you have many men friends then?"

"That is not so. Only Commander Bray, who is my fiancé."

"First-class indeed. So you are a betrothed woman, yet you frequent a house of ill-fame with another man. What are you saying about this one, Memsahib?"

"Don't say any more, Rana," I cut in desperately, "We'll all be in jail when this snooper has got through with us."

Rana turns on me like I was a bag-snatcher. "Don't you dare speak to me, you... you... you dancing-partner you. Commander Bray shall hear of this - then watch out for trouble. I hope you get the biggest hiding of your life...."

This remark actually cheers me up because a lot of people have made it before in all seriousness, such as Fireman Tucker of Southampton and Bandsman Bangle of Chatham - both of whom recovered afterwards - without realizing what they were up against. Hence it is unlikely that a *passé* bridge barker like Bray is going to turn me neurotic with fear.

Strangely enough, when I finally leave Madam Matalia's establishment the only friend I seem to have is the police officer, who escorts me out with the air of a man who has at last found an influential friend to ensure his promotion.

You will not be surprised to hear that everybody is relieved when we are in a state of readiness for putting to sea again - particularly me. After her refit the *Soonong* is brought alongside the jetty for revictualling, but Commander Bray is worried by the fact that his ship has a pronounced tilt as she lies in the water. In fact she is so far down by the nose that a blade of the screw is visible astern, and has such a list to starboard that the gangway from the jetty is hardly long enough to reach her sloping deck. In short she resembles the Fighting Temeraire just before that gallant ship foundered.

It is only this sad state of affairs which takes Commander Bray's mind temporarily off my escapade with Rana. The police report was sent direct to my C.O., who is of course Commander Bray, and its effect on him was not pleasant to behold.

"Everybody is entitled to their bit of fun now and then down the bagnios - but you've gone too far this time, taking my Rana with you, Pook," he lectures me full blast. "I've seen some queer carry-ons in my life but never one that low. I'll never forgive what you done to me this time."

"We were merely trying to buy you a book for your birthday," I explain for the n-th time, but this only makes him worse.

"Shut up, you mouthy liar - at least be a man and admit you pulled the shabbiest trick in the manual. But mark my words, Pook, you'll pay for it even though it costs me my brass hat and I swing from the yard-arm."

"You're too sensitive - that's your trouble," I tell him coldly. When people call me a mouthy liar it's usually the last thing they call anyone for about three weeks.

"And you're too damn impudent, Pook. From now on we speak only in the course of duty - it'll be *sir* this, and *sir* that, got it?"

"You've never called me *sir* before, so why start. . . ?"

"Shut up and clear out."

I should worry. All my life there have been plenty who don't speak to me - mostly the type I'd ignore anyway. Moreover all one gets from Bray these days are unending orders wrapped in the mumbo-jumbo of the sea, difficult to translate and often impossible to perform. As I told him, when he barks orders at me it is a case of an irrepressible demanding the inexpressible of an unimpressible. Nevertheless the condition of the *Soonong* provides a welcome respite in Bray's war of attrition.

Lieutenant (E) Kala, who has been in charge of the refit, recommends the unprofessional solution that more salvage gear should be loaded aft to trim the vessel, but Commander Bray soon discovers that there is a leak amidships. After sealing off the relevant compartment he sends me down from the diving-boat to investigate, with the added rider that he doesn't care if I never come up again.

With characteristic discernmnent I notice that the bow is resting on the bed of the harbour, so I phone the information up to Bray in the terse parlance of duty.

"Oh, glad tidings, Pook," he growls bitterly. "And what, in the opinion of the human crab, is the reason for the nose resting on the bed - and don't you dare tell me the ship's tired."

"There's a leak, sir."

"Good. Good. Always like my officers to tackle a problem from the very fundamentals of human knowledge. Is it a watery leak by any chance? How do you account for such a watery leak, Pook - or am I jumping too far ahead of you? Perhaps first you'd rather go into the question as to whether it's a fresh or salt watery leak, eh?"

"Probably the result of your running the ship aground at Cape Madalla, sir. Left a nasty big hole."

"Good again. Tactless but definite. Now, Pook, before I slash your air-pipe, what do you intend to do about it?"

"Slap a patch on, sir, like I did for the *Kuwain* at Singapore. That soon stopped her list to starboard." Saving the *Kuwain* was one of the best jobs I ever did, and my first experience of patching a hole in a ship's hull. Unfortunately, although I prevented her sinking she caught fire while I was using the underwater blowtorch, with the result that they had to scuttle her eventuallly to put the blaze out.

"Well, Pook, can you do the work without our going into dry-dock? - after all, we can hardly afford to wait another three years for a berth in Chattoo Dockyard."

"Aye definitely aye, sir. I'll use the Lemming bolt-gun same as I did on the *Kuwain*. This way you literally fire the bolts through the hull plates and that's that - patch secured by teatime and liberty boat ashore forthwith."

"Can we have a Lemming bolt-gun flown out from England, Pook?"

"No need, sir. They probably won't have any left because there's eighteen of 'em in our stores."

"Good thinking, lad. Come up and prepare to bolt a blank on the hole tomorrow forenoon."

"With respect, sir, an efficient diver is always prepared for any emergency. I happen to have a bolt-gun lying up topsides in the diving-boat."

"And I suppose you've got a steel blank of the exact size tucked away in your woolly drawers?"

"Actually, my expert examination of the hull tells me that the standard patch stowed in the diving-boat will suffice. All that is needed are eight bolts to hold it in place over the damage. It's really a kind of invisible-mending job with steel stitches if that'll help you grasp the technical side of the operation."

"Very good, Pook, I'll send down the patch and gun at the double."

"Aye aye, sir. Lower away with every confidence."

It would only bore the layman to learn how, humming a traditional diving shanty, I fire the first bolt into the five-eighths-inch plate of the *Soonong,* hang the washer-backed patch on this bolt, then fire seven more bolts through the patch-holes before finally screwing nuts on the bolts and tightening up all round. Suffice to say that it is so expertly done that a patch on a punctured tyre was never more slickly laid on. With justifiable pride I surface to tell Commander Bray he has only to pump out the flooded compartment and we are away.

"You name your trouble, Commander, and I'll fix it," I advise him as I undress in buoyant mood. "Pump her dry then pipe all hands to splice the main brace and all that nautical jazz."

It is not until Friday week when the *Soonong* is in dry-dock that we discover why it is impossible to pump her dry or even to use her own pumps to do it. As Commander Bray remarks, "We've had the dockyard fire-brigade pump half Chattoo Harbour out of the ship yet she's still full - except at high tide, and then the water in her rises. I guess she must be tidal."

Moreover there is a lot of trade jargon going on between Lieutenant Kala and Commander Bray, who cannot understand why they have lost the use of the *Soonong's* engines. There is talk about loss of vacuum and rumours that the steam condenser has packed up. Worse still, Bray starts muttering something technical concerning the circulating water inlet being blocked. It would appear that if this remote piece of apparatus isn't cleared, all form of maritime life ceases. To me it is particularly revolting to learn that one's whole mobility and fighting efficiency depend upon some unspeakable orifice in the hull that one can't even see. Engineering technicalities have always been abhorrent to me ever since my Uncle Paul gave me a construction set as a boy, under the impression that its intricacies would take my mind off girls. I recall pawning it for three shillings and buying a knuckleduster with the proceeds.

"Well, there's one consolation - if the circulating water inlet is blocked then the sea can't be coming in that way," I chaff them cheerfully. I'd help them even further if I knew what the blessed thing is."

"Maybe, Pook, but what we're trying to figure out is why the ship has been paralysed ever since you went below."

"Nothing to do with me, sir - that's the oily-rag department's headache. My job was to bung up the leak."

"But you don't seem to have succeeded, do you, Pook? We're still awash but now we haven't got any steam either. What puzzles me is that it's next to impossible to have a circulating water inlet blocked in a clear harbour like Chattoo."

"Well, if you're so worried about the blessed circulating whatnot, for heaven's sake unblock the thing and have done with it. Probably some fool emptied tea-leaves down it or something."

"You may as well know that it would be very difficult to block an inlet with tea-leaves when that inlet is well below the water-line, Pook."

"Then let me go down and ram a plunger through it. I'm fed up with all these technical excuses for the engines packing up. Why, if our own pumps were operating we'd empty the ship in minutes."

"Unlikely, Pook - considering we've already pumped out twice the *Soonong's* own volume."

"That kind of statistical talk doesn't mean a thing to a diver. Just let me get below for some positive action."

"Get cracking then, Pook. At least it will pass the time and keep you out of the way."

"Aye aye, sir. Tell me where the inlet is located, then we'll lower the boom-boat and get mobile. Probably old newspaper blocking the bend in the U-pipe or something."

Commander Bray heaves a deep sigh and looks at me sadly. "You're supposed to be a naval diver, Pook, not a sanitary inspector. Now take a good squint at this - the inlet is right here," he explains stabbing a blueprint of the *Soonong* with a finger like a hairy parsnip. I have to smile at the coincidence on the blueprint.

"Why, sir, the inlet is exactly where I patched the hole with the bolt-gun. You'd have thought I would have noticed it at the time, but I'll swear there was only the leak-hole there."

Commander Bray buries his head in his hands and seems to brood for several minutes as though the Chaplain has come aboard for Sunday Service. Eventually he says in a resigned voice, "Don't bother to go down again, Pook. Wait till we're in dry-dock, then we'll have a look at your handiwork together."

"Just as you say, sir," I reply smart as paint. "After all, why should we always take the can back for the engineroom's mistakes?"

"Exactly, Pook. Perhaps we'll be able to prise your patch off the circulating water inlet without anyone knowing - we don't want another medal from the Nawab just yet."

TEN

Whether Commander Bray rolls along to his cabin to sedate himself or to dull the edge of his woes via the magga bottle we shall never know, but whatever his trouble he soon formulates a cure. I sense that he keeps brooding over the Rana episode down town, so I deem it politic to lie low as much as possible by dozing the time away in the privacy of the recompression-chamber. Therefore it does not cheer me up to hear his heavy tread lumbering along the deck. Quickly I pretend to be at work by polishing a butterfly-nut on the chamber door and merrily humming a tune in true dockyard style.

"Thought I'd find you skiving in here, Pook," he grunts irritably. I can smell trouble and magga simultaneously.

"Just keeping the gear all shipshape and Bristol fashion," I reply, using the jargon of the sea to put him in better temper.

"Follow me, Pook," he orders in dangerous mood. "There's things to be said and done which won't bear witnessing by the crew, so I guess the jetty is as good a place as anywhere."

He leads me to a deserted quay in front of a godown marked *Salvage Stores - Pumps* and does a strange thing as a prelude to conversation. He rips his gold epaulets off his shoulders and flings them on the cobbles. "Don't let three brass rungs worry you, Pook," he snaps without looking at me. "Not that they ever did in the past, because I'm only 250 pounds of wind and ginger - as I've heard you telling Honners more than once. So I'm going to do you the favour of letting you talk to me as an equal, and we can forget naval discipline for the next half-hour."

"I can't consider you my equal with these on either," I reply, ripping off my own shoulder-straps, "they inhibit me. So now we're a couple of angry civilians again you tell me what's on your mind - *Mister* Bray."

"What's on my mind is that you deliberately bungled that job on the hull of the *Soonong* to keep us in port, all right? Even a curly-headed punk like you couldn't do anything so wet accidentally."

"Keep us in port! I like that! We wouldn't be in port at all if you hadn't rammed the Madalla coast like a week-end sailor on Frensham Ponds. There's more behind it than that, so let's have out with it."

"I'll say there is, Pook. You took it into your head to have a change of girl-friend - I've been watching it. You had it all figured out to get your big maulers on Rana, that's for sure. What you wanted was for me to be sent up to Jawanagar to report on the condition of the *Soonong* - then you'd have a clear channel with Rana while I was up in the hills acting as pen-pal."

"You must be a bigger coconut than they say. Rana! That retarded spinster. She's no good to me because I need more than just a lady's companion. When a man's got the sharpest chicken in port he doesn't go for old boilers until he's senile - that's why she's your girl. Rana is old enough to be Tina's mother at thirty - well over the hill. . . ."

Even in his morose condition I hadn't really expected Commander Bray to clout me, so I am sitting on the cobbles nursing a rapidly-expanding ear. He's still talking . . . "And what's more, if you get up, the senile old boiler-chaser will flop you again."

Even sitting down I radiate confidence born of dormant power. I tell him, "So it's come to this - striking an officer, eh? Surprise attack won't do you any good, Bray. You're too old for me. I'm in enough trouble without being charged with assaulting pensioners. Gooji's more your mark - he's fat and forty too."

Bray bends over me and leers. "The gift of the gab won't save your hide this time, Pook - unless your liver's as yellow as your hair. Up you get."

Now the big fellow is about to help me to my feet but I'm too shrewd a campaigner to fall for the chivalry-bash routine. Instead I rise under my own steam, bury my chin in my shoulder and spar with Bray like I did with Bandsman Bangle at Chatham. It occurs to me that there is more Bray round the waist-line than anywhere else so I let him have the left hook on the belt. Although he gasps harrowingly, the pain motivates his giant arms as though he's been seized by a fit and I am careful to manoeuvre skilfully out of the trap by falling flat on the jetty. He hasn't really hurt me - just that it is unwise to stand up when one's neck seems to be broken.

"Had enough, Pook?" he leers at me, "or are you playing hard to get again?"

I grin up at his thick cabriole legs sportingly. "Guess I underrated you, Bray - you're young at heart really. From now on I'll tan you like you were in my class, so don't plead age when you get what's coming to you."

"Then stand up and patronize me on your feet, you mouthy squirt."

Naturally enough, now I know the score, I toy with him in the boxing line, punching him at will all round the jetty like I did to Bandsman Bangle when we were matched against the Army. This is strictly a merciless process but it has to be done if I am to cut this bulky matelot down to size. Soon his nose is bleeding, his shirt is ripped off, his ginger hair runs with sweat, and ugly patches disfigure his body as though he has scarlet fever. Jaw sagging, he leans against the godown door and gasps defiantly, "Get up, you quitter - and I'll finish you for good and all."

Frankly I am the victim of sheer rough-house tactics that would fell a horse. In any ring Bray would have been disqualified ages ago because he makes up for lack of defence by seizing my arms every time I thump him and cross-buttocks me down on to the cobbles with black-out force. But if he thinks he can win by terrorizing me he is mistaken. I jump up as soon as the nerves in my legs start functioning again, for this time I am resolved to put him away with the big punch and no more free falls.

After softening him up with a short jab to the groin I step in with practised ease to hook him jaw-wise the way I finished Fireman Tucker of Southampton. Now Bray is really in trouble, and in a desperate effort to save himself he knees me in the stomach and rabbit-punches my neck as I fold up.

"That's what we used to call the China Coast double," he informs me as I hit the deck. Although I sense that I have got him going, it seems this is to be the toughest win I ever had. Even during the bout with Bandsman Bangle we used gloves, and Bangle observed some of the Queensberry Rules, whereas the only thing Bray hasn't done yet is bite me.

"Now get off the keel-blocks and finish me," he jeers, "and I'll show you how we fought on the China Coast in the old days."

The maddening part is that I can easily finish him off if only I could get up. I crawl around the cobbles trying to remember how one stands up, but my memory seems to have forgotten this simple operation. "Don't run away - I'm just coming," I boast, stalling for time. "If you want to turn an argument into a prize-fight you picked a wrong 'un."

Eventually I locate a bollard and hoist myself upright like a child in a playpen. I'm not worried really because Bray probably thinks I am foxing him. Following up this angle I box clever, crouching nearly double as if in pain, and breathing heavily as though distressed. My plan is to go for Bray's soft underbelly because hitting him elsewhere is strictly for masochists. In fact my long experience in the ring tells me one of my knuckles is already broken, which could well rob me of victory. My long experience in the ring is also telling me to quit while I am still winning. Even a Service champion of my calibre can't give away fifty-odd pounds and expect to win every trick.

Powerful as he is, a one-two in the stomach reveals to me that age is beginning to count - making me wish he was older than he is. Nevertheless Bray coughs and grunts like a seal in labour, which encourages me to give him a dose of his own medicine. We are grappling so close that I put my arms round his waist to lift him for the cross-buttock, but it is surprisingly difficult to lift a man when your feet are off the ground. In the scrum we appear to be lifting each other, but this is foolish policy for me because, although I am lifting Bray, it is his feet which are on the ground. I sense I have blundered for once.

"Got you at last, you cocky swab!" he shouts triumphantly, bending me concave with a 250-pound purchase. He is so heavy that if he throws me this time it's the breakers for me - so I pretend to faint in his arms like women must do when they dance with him. Surprised, he lowers me to the ground, so on the way down I clout him in the liver good and hard.

Now he is on the cobbles, holding his stomach with both hands without laughing. Advantage to me, but unfortunately I can't exploit it at the moment because he is lying across my head.

"You vicious scab, Pook," he pants. "You'll pay for that if I have to swing for it from the yard-arm." So saying he grabs my throat but the savage expression on his face impels me to jerk free like a bug in a nature film. He is surprisingly fast for an old 'un because he is on his feet nearly as quick as the young 'un, causing me to concentrate solely on keeping out of his grasp in a series of convoy zigzags based on Darwin's self-preservation theory.

Unfortunately he manages to garrotte my throat again with his enormous mauler and swings his free fist at my jaw. Ducking instinctively, I feel the momentum carry him over my shoulders as I go down under his weight, but when I open my eyes again he has disappeared completely. A tremendous double splash tells me he has plummeted some fifteen feet over the edge of the jetty to join his natural habitat the sea.

Peering down, I glimpse his bulk float to the surface face downwards, motionless, so I jump after him feet first. Once in the cool water my head clears, enabling me to turn my victim on his back and keep his face above the surface. Slowly I tow him barge-fashion towards the stone stairs some fifty feet to the right, shouting for help every time I can muster enough wind.

Footsteps aloft indicate that somebody has heard my cries. Then, after what seems a full dog-watch, I glimpse legs running down the slimy green stairs. They are so short that they can only belong to Honners. I don't remember any more.

It is an odd sequel to the most embarrassing experience of my career to be standing once more on the dais of the Presence Chamber in front of the Nawab while he pins the Ramsami Cross to my breast. "For saving life at sea beyond the call of duty," the Nawab drones, reading from the official citation with a noticeable lack of enthusiasm. "Congratulations, Lieutenant Pook - you are indeed a credit to our ancient fighting Service."

"It was nothing really, sir - just luck plus duty, initiative, and native courage. Commander Bray would have done the same to me had the position been reversed," I state frankly. "We were having our customary stroll round the bunder, planning the next salvage operation, when he absentmindedly stumbled over a bollard on the quay. Imagine my dismay to see him unconscious in the water far below me. Naturally, without regard for personal safety I dived to his assistance immediately."

"And cut yourself to ribbons going through the air?"

"No, sir - it was the cruel barnacles on the stairs."

"Those cruel barnacles have left you a sorry sight, Lieutenant Pook. You might have bled to death," the Nawab observes, examining my bandages, puffed ear, cut mouth, and the two brown buns where normally my eyes are stationed.

"But you should see the state Commander Bray is in, sir," I reply, to take his mind off me. The Commander is standing behind me in the audience, wearing a bandage like a turban where his head hit the edge of the jetty.

"Ah, his condition has not escaped my notice, Lieutenant Pook, I assure you. Let us pray that after the war plastic surgery will restore his features to their original shape. Our surgeon who set his hand tells me it is the most remarkable thing in his medical experience - multiple injuries sustained by falling in water. Be so good as to summon the gallant Commander to our presence."

Commander Bray is called to the royal dais where he inspects my medal with his good eye. "You deserve it, Pook, and I forgive you," he mutters sportingly, extending his bandaged hand and shaking my plaster cast.

I accept his apology with good grace. "Don't take it too much to heart, Skipper. You put up a stout show but you can't expect to win them all," I console him.

The Nawab joins us to say, "Ah, gentlemen, how blessed we are that our brave Service is winning so many medals without sighting the enemy," whereupon Bray eyes me strangely.

The Nawab looks at both of us and purses his thin lips. "I believe in your Island Home you have a proverb about taking in each other's dhobi, have you not?"

"It's all in the fortunes of war, sir," I explain hastily. "Part of our job is to help one another besides defeating the enemy."

"And sometimes we get a little mixed up and do both simultaneously, sir," Commander Bray remarks icily.

Just as the interview draws to a close the Nawab takes a package from bis robes and hands it to Commander Bray.

"A small souvenir of the occasion, gentlemen," he purrs. "The Gondah went to the jetty in question to thank Pijee for your deliverance and found these by the door of the godown. We thought you would like to have them for remembrance. Good day, gentlemen."

Commander Bray flips the lid open, to reveal four epaulets, rather the worse for dirt and liberally sprinkled with coconut-oil.

Believe me, shipmates o' mine - if I may be permitted to call my readers by one of Commander Bray's own terms - were I a common scribbler of adventure in foreign parts I could tell you tales so outlandish as to be beyond belief. Tales of voodoo, Tongs, drugs, ruby mines, phantom ships, coral islands, fakirs, temples, and the like which are the staple diet of lesser authors. Not that I haven't had my share of these things but in this story we are concerned with the hard facts of naval life - therefore the tale is plain and down to earth, unadorned with that fanciful atmosphere so far removed from the decks of a man-o-war such as the *Soonong*.

Hence I am in a happy frame of mind when the *Soonong* sails once more from Chattoo. However, my degree of happiness falls sharply when Commander Bray details me as Temporary Welfare Officer, on the grounds that when not actually diving I am the only officer on the ship with no visible employment.

"My being matron to the crew day and night interferes with the running of the ship, Pook," he tells me. "The book says we have to help the men with their problems because a contented ship is an efficient ship - so just you try it and see if it makes you contented and efficient."

"Everybody has personal problems, sir - even me."

"Yes, Pook, even you. But there's problems and problems. Yours are simple ones common to all sexy slobs, but this mob has problems you can't even begin to understand."

"With great respect, sir, that's utter cock and bull. You can break every problem down to three basic factors - cause, effect, cure. Nothing to it really with a smart charlie in the chair."

"You reckon so? Then call in Serang Bundi and see if Aunty Pook can break down his problem."

Serang Bundi waddles into the cabin, salutes and grins broadly. In his hand is a dirty document which appears to have once contained fish and chips. By his side stands one Petty Officer Zalu, our Tindal and interpreter, who professes to be able to establish communication with Bundi's mind in the Shakalese dialect.

"Very bad case this one, Sahib," the interpreter announces solemnly. "Land litigation very worrying, Sahib."

"Then let's have it short and sharp, man," Bray orders.

The two ratings converse at length in Shakalese, gesticulating and head-rolling the while as though watching an air display overhead. "Bundi says his uncle's water is ruining his wife's paddy-field, Sahib. Bundi says by law his uncle's water should drain into his wife's paddy-field, Sahib. Bundi says his uncle has been bribed by his landlord to divert his water to his cousin's paddy-field, Sahib. Bundi says his. . ."

"Simple enough, Commander," I butt in. "The age-old problem of ships and seaman the world over - irrigation of paddy-fields."

Bray glares at me. "Then why does Bundi's chitty say he's worried because he has lost his chakka? Ask Bundi that?"

Interpreter Zalu has a long chat with Bundi about this state of affairs, both men conversing as though engaged in a heated argument about the sky above. Eventually the mystery is solved.

"Bundi says he has lost his chakka, Sahib," Zalu explains triumphantly.

"Then why didn't he report it to the Duty Officer?" Bray demands.

This poser sets Bundi and Zalu wrangling indefinitely. At last enlightenment dawns on the latter's face. "Bundi says his uncle owes him three bullocks, Sahib. Bundi says how can his daughters marry without bullocks for dowry, Sahib?"

"How many daughters has he, for good luck's sake?"

Bundi consults the ceiling and counts on his fingers. "Bundi says eleven by his pukka wives, Sahib."

"What has all this got to do with his chakka?"

"Bundi says three are already married but one is dead, Sahib."

"But surely that is his chakka in his hand."

"No, Sahib, this is his wife's chakka. It is his own chakka he is losing."

"When did he last have his own chakka?"

Zalu and Bundi go into endless conference over this question. The latter points in all directions like a trafficpoliceman with a nervous breakdown. "Bundi says his headman of village is very angry with his uncle for letting his cousin dry up his paddy-field, Sahib. Bundi says his uncle is putting a curse on his wife because she is refusing to pay for his tancha, Sahib. Bundi says how can he have children if his uncle is putting a curse on his wife, Sahib?"

"Which wife?"

"On his third wife, Sahib, whose chakka he is holding."

Commander Bray taps the desk. "Let's start again from the beginning, man. Bundi has lost his own chakka, right? I want to know when and where he lost it and why he has his wife's chakka."

The interpreter questions Bundi closely on this matter, pointing repeatedly at the wife's chakka. Bundi points to the horizon towards Ceylon, then at Burma, and lastly to the South Pole. "Bundi says his wife is again with child, Sahib," Zalu explains.

"But he said just now she can't have any more children because somebody's uncle has put a curse on her."

Zalu looks shocked. "Please, Sahib, I am not understanding. Who is saying this terrible thing?"

"Bundi."

"Oh, no, Sahib, Bundi is not saying this terrible thing."

"Well, you yourself told me he said this terrible thing - is he lying or are you?"

"Bundi does not lie, Sahib. I do not lie, Sahib," Zalu states in a tone indicating that that leaves only the Commander. Zalu and Bundi confer deeply over this collision of facts. Eventually Zalu clears up the matter. "Bundi's uncle declares he is refusing to pay for his own tancha unless his cousin makes good the three bullocks he has lent to his headman."

Commander Bray thumps the desk angrily. "Just you stick to the point and answer me why his wife is pregnant."

"Because Bundi has been to bed with her, Sahib. You yourself signed his leave chitty so he could go to his village on compassionate leave and get his wife's chakka, Sahib."

"So there can't be a curse on her, eh, Zalu?"

Zalu's face lights up as the extent of the Commander's dullness dawns upon him. "Ah, Sahib, this pregnant woman is Bundi's second wife."

"Then what the devil has she got to do with this case?"

"She won't give up her chakka, Sahib. How is the tancha of Bundi's uncle to be paid if she is not giving up her chakka, Sahib? Bundi's cousin is saying that if his bullocks are not returned he is withdrawing his own chakka."

"What will that do? Cause Bundi's camels to urinate?"

"Bundi's uncle will not be having any water, Sahib."

"Why not, in the name of Bedlam?"

"Because the headman is refusing to return these bullocks, Sahib."

"Can't he be forced to?"

"Oh, no, Sahib, because his daughter is pregnant again."

"What has *she* got to do with all this chaos?"

"She is Bundi's first wife, Sahib."

"And she has lost her chakka too, I'm sure."

"No, Sahib, she has given it to Babu, her lover. That is why Bundi's cousin is seeking for tancha from his landlord by-and-by."

Commander Bray turns to me and wipes his forehead with a large handkerchief. "What you have just heard, Peter, is not the case itself but merely the warm-up. Fortunately this is one of the more straightforward problems the men have, so no doubt you'll have it cleared up by the end of the war. Meantime I'll turn the file over to your nimble mind while I bimble about up topsides running the ship. Best of luck to you."

It is soon evident that my duties as Welfare Officer leave me two alternatives. The first is to try and help the ratings while I gradually go off my rocker in the process. The second is to allocate one hour each day for personal interviews and let each man have his fling without interruption until the hour is up - finally ushering him outside, at the same time returning his gestures, shrugs, smiles, and head-waving with one's own gestures, shrugs, smiles, and head-waving.

Rapidly I master the art of Oriental logic - that circular meandering process of delay and side-tracking - until the day comes when I can meet Bundi and Zalu practically on their own ground. I learn to assume an air of eternal patience mixed with hopeless resignation, countering vague issues with even vaguer red-herrings - until the interviews grind slowly to a halt, bogged down in apathy, confusion and misunderstanding beyond extrication by the human mind.

Perhaps my chief aim is to spin out the problems till the end of the commission when Bundi and his messmates will be drafted out of my life for ever, taking with them those insoluble personal problems which dominate their waking hours and fill our office files to bursting point.

One forenoon Commander Bray says to me, "Good work, Pook; you've done a fine job on the Welfare side for the men. Requests to see you are down by two-thirds and the remaining third seem quite cheerfully baffled under your guidance."

"It was nothing really, sir - just routine for a sharp Lieut. sweating on his promotion."

Bray ignores the hint as usual, although sometimes he predicts my next rank will be Able Seaman. "What about Bundi - he ever find his chakka, Pook?"

"To be honest I don't know. At present he's helping me locate mine, which certainly takes his mind off his own troubles. Keen psychology, wouldn't you agree, sir?"

"You mean to tell me you've lost your chakka, Pook?"

"Yes, sir."

"Good heavens."

"All hands waiting to see the Welfare Officer are automatically put on search party fatigue for my chakka, sir, thereby killing twenty-seven birds with one stone, by the last count. This forenoon they are turning out mess stores in case it has dropped down behind the ghee rations."

Commander Bray looks at me incredulously. "Maybe I'm in for a bout of malaria, Pook, but just as a matter of interest do you know what a chakka is?"

"No, sir."

It is one of the extraordinary things about the Royal Ramsami Navy, this bandying about of outlandish terms I can never fathom. Not only is Bundi accumulating new problems set up by his search for my chakka but I don't even know what a chakka is. I am not foolish enough to complicate the issue in Bundi's brain by trying to find out from him.

"Would it paralyse your tiny mind, Pook, if I told you that it is impossible for a European to have a chakka - that only a Ramsami born and bred can possess a chakka?"

"No, sir. All I know is that when I tell the men I've lost mine they all laugh - and laughter is the panacea for mental disorders. Then I tell them to go and look for it, and they march off slightly hysterical. In that way their troubles are cured and I get some peace. I may take up psychiatry after the war, sir - could be I have a natural gift for this sort of guff."

"Are you trying to drive me off my nut, Pook? Can't you be trusted to do damn-all without mucking it up hook line and sinker, when I'm at my wit's end to keep the ship together?"

"Then you should have appointed Lieutenant Kala as Welfare Officer, sir. He's Ramsani and better able to understand the Eastern mind than me. Lately it feels I don't even understand the Western mind any more."

"Thank you, Pook. I am aware that every jerk around here makes the orders and sends them up to the bridge for my benefit, but in this case the men wouldn't wear it. They figure that a Ramsami officer would be prejudiced, whereas a European officer is always fair even if he don't know a blessed thing about the job. That's why I selected you. You may be an idiot at times, but at least you're a just idiot."

"I'm a touchy idiot too - don't forget that."

"All right, Pook - don't let's row again just as things are

getting interesting. There's work to be done, my lad, so I'm taking you off Welfare for the time-being."

"Are the Japs in the, area, sir?"

"No - so thank your lucky stars for that, in this tub. Tomorrow we reach Position 9 on the Pijee chart. What do you think about that?"

"I think it's sheer waste of time. Searching the Indian Ocean for a tuppenny-ha'penny anchor - we must be crackers. If we weren't half doped with the atmosphere of Ramsam we'd be honest and say it was the biggest load of bull ever cooked up in naval history. How you've got the gall to stand there - a full-grown professional seaman - and talk about sending me down on a cock-and-bull assignment like that beats me."

Bray leers at me as though peering through fog. "But you're going down just the same, ain't you, Pook? You know better than disobey an order, don't you, Pook? You wouldn't be the first two-ringer I've put in irons - get that in your head."

"Let me tell you I'm going down merely to relieve the monotony of life with Uncle Bray, nothing more. The sooner I get transferred out of this sea-going temple the better. Money isn't everything and I'd rather be back in Calcutta doing a proper job of work with normal folks connected with the war. I'm fed up with playing at treasure-hunts."

"Watch it, Pook. Under these abnormal circumstances I've let you relax discipline but don't push me too far unless you want to have a liverish bull on your back, like you describes me to Honners. Make the best of it and appreciate which side your bread's buttered on. Who knows, tomorrow you may go down and actually find something like you were a pusser diver and not just a social dilettante in a rubber suit."

"I'll have you know, sir, that I am rather touchy about puerile references concerning my professional prowess under . . ."

"And I'll have you know that the Navy always went under the designation of the Silent Service until you joined it - so close your great bilge-pipe and turn to at the double."

Giving him a sad look I decide to let this pass, and saunter aft to check my gear for another day of fruitless endeavour.

ELEVEN

Although ostensibly the *Soonong* is once again on reconnaissance patrol Commander Bray and Honners check our position over and over again by every device in the book. Honners, who rather fancies himself as an astral navigator, has turned amateur astronomer in his efforts to pinpoint the ship over Position 9 on the chart. He employs the sun, moon, planets and stars in an orgy of figuring, as though navigation is a matter of plotting within a sixteenth of an inch.

Of late his conversation revolves round chronometers, sextants, log-tables, cross-bearings, sets, dead-reckonings, and a host of other technicalities essential to mapping an ocean. When I tackle him about this new-found enthusiasm for navigation he stares at me, as one in a coma. Lately it takes him some time to withdraw his mind from the heavens and focus it upon the trivia of earthly life, but eventually he manages it. "Well, Peter, I see it this way," he explains. "Locating Pijee's Anchor obviously means a great deal to the Ramsamis, so if we ever do it there'll be a generous hand-out in medals, bounties, and promotions. You know I'm strictly a career man, not an itinerant waster like yourself, so what's in it for me? After all, Bray is the head charlie and you're what is humorously known as the diver, so all that's left for me is First Lieut. Now First Lieuts. are notorious for doing the graft like the honorary secretary of a tennis club - but they don't get much kudos and even less of the ball game. Thus I figured that if I want to climb on the bandwagon it's up to me to pinpoint the precise location of the hook."

"Good thinking, Honners. But how will people know you did the donkey work?"

"Exactly, Peter. That's why I've written this, just in case we strike lucky," he replies, handing me a typed script. "This tells the dramatic story of how I located the anchor by astrology. That's the gimmick you need in Ramsam. See, I studied the stars and they led me to Pijee's Anchor. Actually I'm using every trick in the manual but think how this stuff will go down in Ramsam - First Lieut. guided to Pijee's Anchor by following the Zodiac Belt. Not exactly pukka R.N. navigation, but what a Nawab-attracting line! Why, they may even give me an appointment at N.H.Q. as Chief Navigational Seer or something."

"But how will you release your story, Honners? Bray will never stand for it going through the sparker while we're still at sea."

"Simple. Back in Shaggapore my little Shrini has a copy all ready for the *Ramsami Intelligence* the moment anything breaks. I reckon that alone is worth a few thousand rupees on the side."

"Good luck, pal. You'd live in luxury where others starve."

Thanks to Honners' mathematical efforts we are able to lower the diving-boat at 8 a.m. on one of those ideal forenoons when the waters of the Indian Ocean are so hot and still that it seems you could walk over the surface. As the depth is fifteen fathoms we have two pumps in readiness and a trainee-diver dressed in case I become foul or need assistance. Commander Bray, anxious to eliminate mistakes, insists we do everything this time according to the book, as we have rehearsed so many times in training.

Dressed in the suit, boots, and corselet I stand smartly to attention on the iron ladder while Petty Officer Zalu screws down the helmet, then makes fast the weights. When I am satisfied that the air is coming through nicely he screws on my front glass and taps the helmet with his hand to signal me to dive. He is holding my breast-rope, Bundi has charge of the air-pipe, and the pump is being hove round in an efficient manner, so down I go, leaving the ladder to continue my descent on the shot-rope.

Despite the number of successful dives I have made in the past the experience of entering the unfamiliar world below never ceases to entrance me. Today the light is excellent, enabling me to see clearly the many forms of fish life which populate these waters in such profusion. Always when first reaching the sea-bed the feeling strikes me of alighting on an unknown planet such as Venus, but these thoughts are soon forgotten as the routine search occupies my attention.

This forenoon my eyes are drawn to a shadowy shape just within my range of vision to starboard of the *Soonong*. Straightway I trudge slowly towards it until I reach the limit of my distance-line. At this point the shape still seems far away, but for my money it appears too symmetrical to be the normal coral formations I have come to know so well. Eventually I break silence by phoning up the news to Commander Bray.

"Maybe it's the hull of the *Soonong* or its mirage," he surmises. "Strange things occur when the sun is high and the water smooth as quicksilver. Nevertheless your description suggests a wreck, although nothing is marked on the chart. Come up just the same while we have a look-see."

Having taken a careful bearing on the shape I ascend and stand down for the search. "If we had another vessel handy we could sweep the area," Bray thinks aloud, "but as we haven't we'll try to inch up on your bearing and hope for the best."

In actual fact the object is much further nor'east than we had anticipated because we don't locate it until the *Soonong* has anchored three times. Directly the news spreads there is considerable excitement among the crew. The Gondah in particular is leaning over the port rail, slowly waving a palm-tree bough as though he is fanning the sea.

"Must think he's some kind of water-diviner," I remark as Zalu and Bundi prepare me for another dip. This time there is no mistaking the object, so close is it to my shot-rope. Eagerly I make towards it and once there the feel of my fingers against wood confirms that this is a very old wreck. I report up to Commander Bray, who orders me to return to the diving-boat.

"Good shooting, Peter," he says, "but it can wait for tomorrow. The sun is below the horizon so we don't want any accidents. Come up and talk things over."

While we are drying the diving-dress and stowing gear for the night Commander Bray has been in contact with N.H.Q. Their reaction at base is surprising to say the least. Commodore Gooji's voice is almost incoherent with emotion as he tells our skipper that he is to be put in direct radio communication with the Nawab himself, and all N.H.Q. are to be alerted for more information.

"You'd think we'd located the blessed anchor itself by the way they're panicking back at N.H.Q.," Bray remarks as we eat supper around the transmitter. "I'm the biggest fool to have signalled our find so soon. The Nawab can't understand why we don't work a night shift on the wreck. He keeps harping on about you going down with a torch as if we were searching the palace cellars."

By midnight Commander Bray clamps down the radio, on the grounds that there just isn't any more one can say about the wreck. Nevertheless, signals continue to arrive, instructing us to dive at sun-up and provide N.H.Q. with a running commentary on everything we see or find. The most unrealistic signal so far - which has Bray beating his great fists on the bulkhead - is one recommending we tow the wreck back to Chattoo Harbour.

Before we finally turn in for the night Bray remarks to me, "Funny thing, Peter - they've fallen over backwards in their excitement about an old wooden wreck, yet have you noticed something odd?"

"Of course. They don't mention a word about Pijee's Anchor."

"Exactly."

"Maybe they assume the hook must be in the vicinity of the wreck, hence a night of great joy in Ramsam."

"I wonder. Just the same I'll check with the Nawab tomorrow."

"Then don't forget to tell him I did all the navigation," Honners reminds him emphatically. "Remember - only teamwork got us on to this wreck, so give me a plug, *Captain* Bray."

Five-thirty next morning the team really goes into action. Honners' job is to lay the diving-boat well off the stern of the *Soonong* by a hawser so that I can go down for the purpose of fixing a sweep wire direct from the *Soonong* to the wreck. Next, we drop a sliding shackle from the diving-boat on to the diagonal sweep wire, thus forming a kind of right-angled triangle between the wreck, the *Soonong,* and the diving-boat, with the latter directly over the wreck. By this method we are enabled to keep the diving-boat right above the wreck whatever the set of the tides, with the ship and the wreck as our fixed points. As an added precaution we put down a marker buoy in case of losing the wreck's position through rough weather. I don't understand the technicalities either, but Bray does - and the chief thing is that it works.

On my first descent to make the sweep wire fast to the wreck I come down on the stem of the vessel and almost at once I spot the anchor. The wreck is lying over at such an angle that it is easy for me to stand upright on the stem to make fast the wire round the stem itself, but all the time I keep glancing at the anchor in case it disappears. From my position it seems to be embedded in the timbers, so directly the wire is secured I scramble the short distance to the anchor itself.

Although it is encrusted with barnacles there is no mistaking the shape of the precious bower-anchor which I saw in the woodcut drawing the Nawab gave to Bray. The action of time has made it almost part of the hull but I figure that with care it can be prised free. Excitedly I phone the news up above.

"Forget the wreck, Peter, and concentrate on the anchor," Commander Bray barks over the line. "Commodore Gooji has already told me over the radio that Pijee's Anchor must lie in the vicinity of the wreck."

"And at the moment I'm sitting on the joker, sir," I chuckle triumphantly.

"Then keep sitting while we send you what you require. Name your tools quickly and I'll send them down on the jackstay."

"Let me have a lifting wire, two crowbars, and a 12-pound hammer fast," I tell him. I don't believe in finesse at a time like this.

As soon as the tools come down the jackstay I tackle the job with zest and skill. Although it seems I can prise the hook out of the timber I don't want to break the cow after all we've been through. Therefore I take the safer course of driving the crowbars into the timber and levering out the anchor and rotten wood together. When it is nearly free I remember the precaution of taking a few turns round the shank with the lifting-wire and reef-knotting the ends rather than risk losing the prize down in the sea-bed. Immediately the anchor is free I phone back the hot news and tell them to haul up carefully. Feeling tired but satisfied I ascend to the diving-boat to witness the historic occasion in comfort.

To say the arrival of the anchor creates a sensation among the crew is sheer understatement. It would be nearer the truth to record that they go crazy with joy, although I must admit the sight of the rusty old piece of ironmongery does not really flood my soul with ecstasy. The Gondah is running about like a worried hen, salaaming, praying, and crying simultaneously. He won't allow anyone to touch the sacred hook, not even himself - which immediately sets up a difficult problem for us in the way of shifting it. He decrees it must stay where it has been landed inboard on deck. The area is roped off and a guard posted round it as if it is radio-active. The Ramsami ratings erect a canvas canopy over it and light some candles, but as these blow out the idea has to be abandoned.

"What a shambles on the deck of a man-o-war," Commander Bray growls to me. "We're not so much a warship as a floating shrine. If it wasn't for the money each month I'd boot the whole shebang overboard - but I'll tell you one thing for sure; if ever some big-mouthed nut takes it into his head after the war to write a book about this lot and make me the laughing-stock of every wardroom in the Royal Navy I'll personally disembowel the slob with my bare bands."

The mere idea tickles me. "You're on a safe bet there, Skipper, none of us can write."

"That don't mean a thing these days, Pook."

Honners is in high spirits. He has sent a cable to Shrini which contains the usual clause that he loves her eternally, but it also contains a new one to the effect that she is to deliver the groceries forthwith. By return comes her confirmation that the aforesaid groceries have been faithfully delivered.

"Didn't realize you were in the beans and bacon business, Honners," Commander Bray remarks, who has to censor all cables.

Honners turns up his nose in disgust. "The Pilkington-Goldbergs have been concerned with many outlandish pursuits, sir, but they have never engaged in trade - it's just not done in our set."

"Then what's all this bilge about delivering the groceries?"

"Charity, sir - simple human charity, with which you of course will not be familiar. A small token of assistance to gentlefolk in reduced circumstances."

"Sounds more like code to me, Honners."

"Which is the logical deduction of a parochial mind. With great respect, sir, thank heaven I am not like other men who put money before everything else. Money - that insidious red-herring which blinds man to the broad panorama of true life."

"Who mentioned anything about money, Honners?

Honners appears confused as he searches around for a side-tracking answer but fortunately Bray is called to the blower. It is Commodore Gooji, who is so excited that he sounds as though he is arguing with himself at the other end. "Wonderful work, Commander Bray," he splutters. "The whole of N.H.Q. is afire with delight at your achievement. Over one hundred years we are waiting for Pijee's Anchor to be returned to us, and to think that I am living to see it. What an unprecedented triumph for the ancient Ramsami art of navigation by astrology."

"Navigation by what?" Bray butts in incredulously.

"Ah, excuse me please, Commander Bray, here is coming the Nawab personally himself to speak with you . . . over."

The Nawab's slow voice comes on the air sounding very matter of fact after the emotional Commodore Gooji. "Greetings, Taurus the Bull - this is Leo the Lion speaking to you from Ramsam, the epicentre of the Zodiac."

"What in the name of - ?" Bray gasps.

"Our people are amazed to read in the *Ramsami Intelligence* how Sagittarius the Arrow directed your ship Aquarius the Water Carrier to Position 9, thus enabling Pook the Crab to enter the world of Pisces the Fish and find Pijee's Anchor."

"What the devil is all this drivel, sir? Are you trying to pull my paying-off pennant or something?"

"How wise of you to choose a day when the stars foretold - I quote from the article - that something important lay beneath your feet waiting your attention; a day full of promise that would affect your future career and bring an increase of a monetary nature; a day when a dark gentleman would hear news to gladden his heart; a day which would provide a sheet-anchor against adversity."

"Are you in your right mind, sir?" Bray demands angrily, "or has one of us been resorting to drugs?"

"My mind has certainly not been improved by reading an account of your astrological navigation in the *Ramsami Intelligence* almost before the news had reached me in a top secret report from yourself, Commander Bray."

"Read about it in the papers? Why, we only located the hook this forenoon. Who wrote the article, that's what I want to know?"

"One Sagittarius the Arrow, the Interpreter of Direction."

"Then it's obviously a hoax, sir. A newspaper stunt in my opinion."

"Should we not rather call it a newspaper stunt arising from a breach of internal security, eh, Commander Bray?"

"Call it what you like, sir - it's nothing to do with me."

"Undoubtedly that will come out when you appear at the official Inquiry along with your junior officers."

"Oh, gawd!"

"Nevertheless, Commander, allow me to congratulate you on your success. In itself a remarkable achievement."

"Thank you, sir. I presume we are to return immediately to port with the old hook."

"Ah, but of course. We cannot have our precious old hook too soon, you understand? However, as you are in situ, so to speak, you may as well investigate the ancient wreck. Let Pook enter the hold to see if there are any relics of the past for our museums; old guns, instruments of torture, coins - gold perhaps. If he finds nothing within the next seven days report to me personally for further orders."

"Seven days! He can comb it in a forenoon, sir. It's not the *Warspite* you know."

"To be precise she is of 780 tons burthen - a far cry from the mighty *Warspite.*"

"You know about her then, sir?"

"I quote from the ancient document in front of me at the moment."

"What is her name, sir?

"Mind your own business."

"A good name for a ship, sir."

"Exactly. I see we understand one another, Commander Bray."

"Good night, sir."

At breakfast next day our skipper relays the news to us in liverish mood, adding, "I don't know if one of you clevercuts is Sagittarius the Arrow, Interpreter of Direction, but whoever he is he's made me look a king-size charlie. When I do find out I'll keel-haul him afore he's flogged round the Fleet. Then we'll check his horoscope to make sure it's his lucky day full of unexpected little joys - and shoot the mouthy punk."

For some reason Honners pushes his plate away untouched, looking pale enough for seasickness. Commander Bray continues, "The Nawab wants us to search the wreck for relics, starting today - and that's top secret, or should I say between you, me, and the *Ramsami Intelligence?*"

"Oh, lovely!" I sneer loudly. "What a war-effort. In years to come my kids will ask me what I did to win the war and I'll say,

'Daddy found a rusty old anchor. Then he looked for souvenirs in a wreck which sank a hundred years ago - that's how he won the pretty medals on his barrel-organ.'"

"That'll be enough of the mutiny chat, Pook. See you get submerged by 0900 hours, understand?"

"Aye aye, sir."

Searching a wreck is always risky work even to an experienced craftsman like myself because there is the danger of falling into deeper water suddenly, thus increasing pressure to danger-point, not to mention fouling one's air-line around obstructions. But at least it's interesting, with the ever-present thought of stumbling across a bit of loot. This is my first experience of working a wreck, therefore I am bewitched by the beauty of the scene.

Although the poop and forecastle have long since disappeared, the hull itself is still intact, covered with kelp weeds and encrusted with shellfish of every description. Here and there I see evidence of teredo-eaten timbers which are quite twisted by the extent to which the vessel has fallen over on her beam-ends. Sufficient of the decks remain to make it necessary for me to crawl through hatches to reach the hold itself, and once inside I lose the light of the sun, finding myself in darkness. Fortunately I have available not only a hand-torch but also a 3,000-candle-power lamp to solve the problem, so, with the help of a crowbar, I begin the task of sorting over the debris all around.

Once one becomes accustomed to their encrusted shapes it is surprising how many objects one can identify. Musket-shot by the dozen; a 25-pounder cannon; tools, a sword, kitchen utensils, bones - all there for the patient searcher. As far as possible I make a pile of everything portable that comes to light, and note the position of heavy equipment such as capstans and carronades which have accumulated down in the hold as the decks collapsed over the years. I keep Honners in touch by phone so that he can record each item as it is located.

Well aft are a number of old chests of such robust construction that they can hardly have been used for stowing gear or carpenter's tools. They are heavily padlocked and so weighty as to be quite immovable unless I use the crowbar as a lever. By the light of the torch it occurs to me that they look very much like pictures I have seen of specie-boxes recovered from one of the galleons of the Spanish Armada. All told there are eleven of these chests, so I report direct to Commander Bray for instructions.

"Don't smash them open, Pook," he warns me as though I have lost my temper, "otherwise any valuables they may contain will be scattered beyond finding. Let's heave one up and investigate."

Bray laughs over the phone with such power that my head sings in the helmet. "This sounds like the real thing, Peter. I'll send down a steel net so the chest won't stave in when we hoist, then we'll winch it up gently. What's your estimate of weight?"

"All of two hundredweight apiece, sir."

"Fair enough. Handle it gently and take your time."

"Aye aye, sir. You know me - always ahead of the next man when it comes to a ticklish job. Rely on me for expertise and fast results so stand by to go about, as we say on the bridge. What do you want me to do first, sir?"

"Shut up."

Believe me, it takes plenty of time to salvage this chest. It's bad enough levering the thing to the net but that is easy compared with steering it clear of the sloping hatch. By the time I have seen it through without fouling the jagged deck timbers I've really had enough. After such exertion I ascend very slowly to give my body a chance to get rid of nitrogen in the blood, then I rendezvous with Commander Bray. He is in jubilant mood because when our blacksmith forces the chest he knows he is on to something big. So big that the Gondah, who has to supervise the opening, is completely overcome. Slowly sinking down with much rolling of eyeballs and incoherent mutterings, he finally succumbs to the spectacle and we have to lay him out flat on his back as if he has received bad news from home. Whether he has fainted or entered a trance is difficult to judge but he is soon forgotten as Bray yanks the contents out of the chest and places them on the deck. Everything is covered with slime and crustacea so he scrapes here and there with a knife.

"Either gold or brass," he decides calmly, "but judging by the weight I'll plump for gold."

"Your servant, sir," I bow modestly, to remind him who found such loot.

By now we have sorted out all kinds of regalia, chalices, chains, tablets, candlesticks, and several unidentifiable emblems, plus a little casket containing rings inlaid with stones.

Commander Bray looks pensive. "Pook, take all this stuff to my cabin and have Honners help you. Post a sentry outside while I have a word with Ramsam. This report had better go straight to the Nawab himself."

The Nawab receives the news with unexpected calm. Pleased, yet not over-excited. "Excellent work, Commander Bray," he drones in that slow nasal voice of his after hearing brief details. "Most gratifying - our endeavours have not been in vain. How many chests remain in the wreck?"

"Ten, sir. Pook has checked carefully."

"Ten, eh? That is a pity - there should be twelve all told."

This really has Bray puzzled. "You mean to say you know all about the trove, sir?"

"Hush. Waste no time in retrieving the other chests. Have Pook work as long as his endurance will permit - tell him his efforts shall not go unrewarded - and emphasize that all the while he must be vigilant for one more chest."

"Aye aye, sir."

"One last detail, Commander - or should I say Captain - Bray, I shall take it kindly if you will keep this affair of the chests completely secret. Naturally there will be much excitement everywhere but this will be on account of the miraculous recovery of Pijee's Anchor, you understand? Play down the treasure angle, to use your delightful English phrase, and let the gold pass into my hands almost unnoticed as it were. Do I make myself clear?"

"Very good, sir, but unfortunately the Gondah had to be present when the chest was opened."

"Oh, I see," the Nawab replies thoughtfully. "What did he say?"

"Nothing, sir. He passed out."

"Hmm - awkward but not insurmountable. Well, Commander Bray, leave that matter to me - your chief concern is the recovery of the remaining chests."

Resuming work on the wreck, I quickly discover that the sample chest happened to be one of the lightest. Rather than kill myself guiding them through the hatch I take down a small charge of dynamite and blow a hole clean through the deck so that the lifting-wire from above can have direct access to the hold. Nevertheless nearly a week passes before all eleven chests are safely on board the Soonong.

In the absence of instructions to the contrary, Commander Bray carefully forces each chest open for a quick check on the contents before sealing them with wax. The finds are staggering. Only two boxes contain ornaments and regalia; three are full of gold coins of all nationalities, while the remaining six are stowed with gold ingots, each one some twelve inches long and four inches wide. All are crudely shaped.

"My guess is that whoever made these was in a hurry," Bray

decides after he has sealed the last chest. "Probably melted down everything valuable in sight and then crated them up. I've seen gold ingots before but never as rough as this lot."

"And had to bung the oddments into the other chests fast," I yawn wearily. The excitement of the treasure has subsided, leaving me dead-beat with fatigue.

"Great pity you couldn't find the missing chest, Pook," the Commander adds tactlessly.

"Probably the crew had to take to the boats when the ship sank, so they carted off the odd chest for petty cash."

"Most unlikely, Pook. If you're sinking you don't lug a two-hundredweight chest up topsides and dump it in a lifeboat with a merry cry of 'Women, children, and loot first.'"

"Then all I can say is the mermaids must have knocked the thing off," I tell him irritably. "There's nothing else down there. By now I know every nut and bolt like it was my home - even the fish recognize me. After all, I've found the biggest cache in years yet everybody seems more concerned with the little bit I can't trace. You want jam on it, mate."

It really irks me the way the Nawab keeps moaning over the lost chest as though it means more to him than all the others put together. Worse still, Bray won't let me have any perks out of the specie boxes. Instead, Honners and I have to witness the official sealing as though our hands have been amputated.

Always in the past I've done pretty well in the rake-off line, and even when I accidentally set the Kuwain on fire whilst sealing a hole in her side at Singapore I managed to appropriate a case of Scotch as she foundered. "How in the name of Pijee is anyone going to miss a handful of doubloons and louis-d'ors out of all that lot?" I demand angrily. "No one's waiting back at Chattoo ready to tick the stuff off on an invoice like it was tins of fruit."

"Ah, Pook, you never know with the Nawab. In any case that's not pusser Admiralty procedure with treasure."

"Then I'm only sorry I didn't accidentally bust the odd box down in the wreck. It's time someone else did himself a bit of good around here."

"Maybe you salted away the missing chest for a rainy day, eh, Pook?"

This remark is so naive that I throw it away, but not so far that it can't be exhumed next time we have our character analysis prior to a row. To date all I've got out of this trip is a snuff-box, a musket-ball, a sore back, and older. Our conversation is interrupted by a call to the S.D.O. for parley with the Nawab. He is in high spirits about the safe recovery of the chests although he still can't understand how I missed one.

"Are you positive you looked in the, cellars and upstairs, Lieutenant Pook?" he demands, as though one of his palaces has sunk in mid-ocean.

"Everywhere, sir - even in the garden," I tell him patiently. "You must bear in mind that the stuff's been down there a long time, sir."

"Very true, Pook, over a hundred years - but it was in Ramsam much longer than that, and we never lost a cent."

This I can well believe but refrain from comment. "You mean the treasure came from Ramsam in the first place, sir?" I fish hopefully. When it involves state finance, news is hard to come by.

"Of course. It is the Pijee ceremonial regalia and the Toolu Temple funds - but this is top secret information between myself and yourself, Pook. Anyone foolish enough to disclose such business of state could easily lose his head."

"But how did so much booty come to be seaborne in the Indian Ocean, sir?" I inquire in my humility voice. What an object lesson in how to pump a summit man.

"Ah, my boy, cast your mind back to 1824, the time of the first war between the Burmese and the British. Quite correctly we of Ramsam anticipated that the British would win because, as you will agree, one cannot conquer half the earth without winning most of the time. Consequently my prudent ancestors melted down many of our treasures and shipped them to the comparative safety of Nagar Kutupos Island. Not that we mistrusted the British of course; let us rather say that we did not wish to put temptation in their way. The British have always been celebrated for their fair dealings abroad, annexing only the territory in question and leaving the wealth of the country untouched so that their merchants would have something to retire on."

"But how come the ship sank, sir?"

"Well, Pook, as you know, we Ramsamis have never been the best sailors in the world so you will not be surprised to learn that our treasure galleon foundered before it reached its destination. It seems there is no escaping the British lion."

"But how did your countrymen know this, sir?"

"Ah, Pook - a great secret of state indeed, involving Pijee's Anchor and the revelations of our mystic Gondahs. When the ship foundered the Great Gondah, who was on board to guard the treasure personally, took possession of the captain's logbook. Now, as a sailor yourself knows, it is child's play to ascertain latitude accurately but a very difficult business to reckon longitude, particularly with the crude chronometers of the period. Consequently for the past hundred years our Gondahs have studied the ancient log in an endeavour to calculate the precise longitude of the disaster in the light of more modern methods. The final bearing agreed upon was the one entrusted to Commander Bray, so now we pride ourselves on the accuracy of our computations."

"But why the emphasis on finding Pijee's Anchor, sir, yet no mention of the treasure?" This is the 64 rupee question, I figure.

There is a long pause before the Nawab answers, and I think I hear a slight chuckle at the other end. Maybe he is wondering how to translate "Nawab's perks" from the Ramsami dialect.

"You see, Lieutenant Pook, we have a maxim in Ramsam which says 'No point in making keyhole bigger than door,'" he explains.

Ramsami adages always fox me. Some of them are quite clever but they appear to have no connexion with the circumstances they are supposed to cover. For example, when I used to woo Kulima, Commodore Gooji would quote with monotonous regularity "When white man make love, price of camel dung go up." Nothing is more calculated to drive romance from one's mind I found.

"I don't really follow you, sir."

"Ah, Lieutenant Pook, you are not so dull as they say. The Anchor is of great religious significance to my people, but the treasure - who is interested in the relics of a bygone age?"

"You for one, sir?" I suggest brightly. If he wishes he can have a list of other interested parties, with my name at the top.

"So, Lieutenant Pook, enough of your delightful nonsense. Please ask Commander Bray to speak with me."

"After all, sir, I found the loot so don't forget your humble servant, sir. Cast your bread upon the waters, sir ...."

The Nawab cuts me short with new urgency in his voice. "Commander Bray immediately, Pook. As we speak, matters of great import have come to hand. Delay not a second more. It is a case of life and death. . . ."

TWELVE

After our skipper has conversed with the Nawab on the radio he is unusually quiet. Apparently we are to drop everything, abandon the wreck and proceed forthwith to Chattoo with the anchor and treasure. There is no further mention of the missing chest so I assume that the Nawab has decided to cut his losses and be satisfied with a fortune.

In the wardroom Commander Bray hints that the Japanese are not so far away as he would wish.

"Just our luck, sir, to be captured or sunk precisely at the moment when I have salvaged the biggest treasure ever recovered in the East," I remind him over lunch. "Rapid promotion won't do me much good if it's going to be confirmed posthumously."

Commander Bray sips his beer thoughtfully. "Thank you, Pook. We're all grateful even awed - to serve in the same ship as yourself and to realize what you've done for us. We can only trust that we haven't been too much of a nuisance to you, getting in your way as you steered the ship, controlled the crew, did the navigation, manned the galleys, and all the other little chores which went on when you weren't actually diving. So now take it easy and try to think more about yourself while the silly old passengers you've been carrying try to sail the ship back to Chattoo as best they can. Just you go lie in your cabin so that we can return to base without incident, happy in the thought that if anything goes wrong we are free to come knocking at your door for advice. Once safely in port everybody will congratulate you, tell you what a wonderful diver you are, give you another medal, and finally boot you clean out of the Service."

"Another medal! I salvage gold beyond the dreams of avarice and you sit there telling me I'll get another gong. I should have thought there'd be at least a ten per cent cut in it for me. Medals are chicken-feed - why, they even gave me one for saving you."

"Let's get back to port in one piece, Peter, before we worry about rewards," Honners chips in. "All I hope is that if we meet the Japanese Grand Fleet we don't do a Drake and attack it single-handed with our 4-inch blazing defiance at it."

"And the Gondah bombarding their Zero carriers with his lethal rice."

"Better to surrender quietly and come to terms about the treasure over a glass of saki in Tokyo, eh? Remember the old Ramsami motto, 'If at first you don't succeed, give up.'"

Commander Bray lights a cigarette and grins at us both. "That's my worry, lads. I shall carry on in the best naval tradition whatever the set of the tide."

"It's my worry too, sir," Honners says apprehensively, "especially as the Japs could sink us without firing a shot - all they need do is steam by and we'd go down in their wash."

"That's not like you, Honners, after all we've heard about the exploits of the fighting Pilkington-Goldbergs - dying like flies for their country down the ages."

"So they did, sir, but not one of them was drowned. They were all in the Army. Legend has it that should a PilkingtonGoldberg be lost at sea the family name will be wiped out."

"How come, Honners? Surely you don't believe that old wives' tale?"

"Oddly enough I do, sir," Honners confesses miserably, "and so would you if you were the last of the male line and stuck on board this old tub in enemy waters."

Although the journey home proceeds quite uneventfully, a very strange turn of fate overtakes us. Almost without warning we discover one day that we appear to be out of radio communication with Ramsam, either by voice or morse. It seems most eerie, because this is the first time the insistent link from N.H.Q. has been broken, rather like a husband whose wife has nagged him for years until the day he wakes up to find her gone. To us the silence is uncanny.

"Obviously the transmitter has been overworked and now it's gone for a burton," I advise Commander Bray authoritatively. "Directly they've done a repair job the short-wave band will be flooded once more with the usual claptrap."

"May be, Pook, but I don't like it all the same. They've got transmitters to spare up at N.H.Q., plus a private station at the Nawab's palace. What really worries me is that Radio Ramsam is also off the air."

"Let's check elsewhere. Why not try Calcutta to see if they have contact with Ramsam?"

"That has already occurred to me, Pook. We're waiting for an answering signal right now."

By this time we are all worried, especially Honners who turns our thoughts to more personal matters by mentioning Shrini, Tina, and all our other friends. "Maybe the Japs have cut through North Burma and entered Ramsam by the back door," he reflects gloomily.

No sooner has he uttered these words than the signal arrives from Calcutta. It does not offer much comfort: "No contact with Ramsam 24 hours. Japanese last reported in vicinity of eastern frontier."

Commander Bray looks extremely grave. "There's no disguising the fact that there's little hope for Ramsam," he remarks.

"If the Japs have broken through as close as that it will be all up, but I'm afraid the radio silence means that they have already seized the country itself."

"So we're a ship without a nation to belong to," I muse soberly. "What a situation to be in."

"It's even more ironical, Pook, when you realize that we were supposed to be on patrol reckying for the Jap Fleet, yet the devils have come through by land."

Bray's interpretation of the situation is confirmed by a signal we receive from Calcutta at 1300 hours. "Ramsam definitely in Japanese hands. No further information at present."

This final confirmation really sends our morale down to zero, especially Honners who takes it very much to heart. But worst of all is our inability to obtain any news of the good people we have come to love so well. Although I am not the worrying kind I can't help wondering what has happened to Tina.

"It just goes to show that in this so-called world of civilization there's no room for little medieval backwaters like Ramsam." Honners declares bitterly. "Unless you're one of the big boys you get trodden out of existence - I should know because I'm only a little 'un myself."

"Let's dump the treasure some place, same as the old pirates used to do, and then go in Commando-fashion up the coast from Chattoo - like we would if we were still in the Royal Marines," I suggest. Being on the *Soonong* is beginning to make me feel lonely and yearn for the old days in the Royals when we were either grovelling in the mud prior to storming something or else marching up the Mall with white topees and bags of bull.

Commander Bray dismisses the notion with a wave of his fist. "I'm still in command here despite the situation ashore - remember that. My mind is already made up. As captain, my duty is to take my ship safely to the nearest friendly port - and that is exactly what

I intend to do. We change course and head for India as from now."

India must be my land of destiny, so many times have I been drafted to it, visited it, convalesced in it, court martialled by it, wrecked on it, and retreated to it. Even back in '41 on an air flight to China we were diverted to it and finally pancaked on it.

Up on the bridge Bray and Honners do some hasty figuring on the charts to work out our best course for clearing the danger zone and slipping quietly across to India's eastern seaboard. For the first time we maintain a discreet radio silence because the news bulletins from Radio Delhi speak of a two-pronged thrust by the Japanese Fleet, one apparently aimed at Ceylon and the other towards India, uncomfortably close to our own position.

"Not a hope, Honners - with the monsoon blowing nor'east like sin we'll never make it to Calcutta without refuelling," Bray decides after a wind and distance check. "The first consideration is to reach safety, so our best bet is Vizagapatam on the Golconda Coast. That's the shortest, safest route - roughly due west from here - then the monsoon won't bother us overmuch. In fact we can use the sails to good advantage."

Honners relays this news to me and I hear it with some misgivings. Serving in the Royal Ramsami Navy has already set in motion an idea in my head wherein the main objective is retiring from the sea permanently. Even in fine weather the old *Soonong* creaks as if she is made of potato crisps undergoing intolerable stress. In foul weather she yaws badly but to me the terrifying thing is the way she pitches. Although a drama of the sea is scarcely the place in which to talk about lavatories, I must confess that I have given up using the officers' toilet right aft in bad weather. The thing is not so much a seat as a launching-pad, giving one the feeling as the stern seesaws some forty feet that you are being thrust up into space by your backside, to be finally flung clear of the earth's gravitational pull. However this is illusory, for after a short period of weightlessness at the zenith you fall back to earth with the blood bursting your head, ready to be catapulted upwards once more. As Honners remarked during a gale, "No man in his right mind would use the place, but if he does it's just as well it is a toilet."

Just such a storm hits us *en route* for Vizagapatam, with disastrous results. This is the dreaded Ezooti one hears so much about in Ramsam when the old hands are talking about winds which have flattened them in years gone by. They say that by comparison the Peyana is a mere breeze alongside the dreaded Ezooti, and this I can well believe. The latter is not so much a wind as Nature's answer to the hydrogen bomb. Certainly I have never experienced the like anywhere in the world, nor have the crew who lie groaning about the decks as though cyanide has been added to the curry accidentally. The stronger members stagger along the guide-ropes like drunkards leaving a party. All is noise and chaos.

"Nasty bit of a blow on," Commander Bray observes to me as the fore-peak ploughs under a wave submarine-fashion. "This is the real navy to me - fighting every inch against the elements. The mizzen-mast's gone over the side, you know."

He tells me this grim news as though it should please me as much as it does him. He is actually laughing. "Cheer up, shipmate - a coward dies a thousand deaths, but only one for me so long as I'm at the helm. Blow, you bastard, blow!"

As he is not looking at me but at the heavens I assume he is addressing the wind, so I stop blowing. I find this primitive delight in the elements most distasteful, particularly at the moment when the only thing between me and a violent end is a load of substandard teak and rust.

"How is Honners, shipmate?" Bray inquires as his order for more wind is granted. All this shipmate business irks me, being redolent of terrible disasters at sea so vividly portrayed in the

Victorian engravings we had at home in the parlour, wherein sailors vied with each other for the honour of drowning in the name of Empire.

"Semi-conscious, sir. I've wrapped him in a sail and lashed him on deck 'midships."

"Best place for seasickness, shipmate. Does he want anything?"

"Wants to die, sir. Muttered something about a farewell message to Shrini in his cabin."

"Rubbish. He'll be as fit as sin come dawn. Did you give him a pill?"

"Tried to, sir, but he's strictly expellent at the moment. It came up like an airgun-pellet."

"How did a little fellow like that ever get in the Navy, Pook?"

"Special qualifications, sir - an uncle at the Admiralty."

"Looks like his dream of a career in the Ramsami Navy has gone up the spout, Pook."

"You really think so? Is it so irrevocable?"

"Seems to me the day of the little autocratic states is over, Pook. Sad, but that's the price of modern life. The big Powers are so big that when they clash the small fellows get crushed between their fenders and the jetty. A great pity, to my way of thinking."

"Maybe it was too good to last, eh, sir? One thing, I enjoyed every moment of it so that's something for the memory album. Even now the whole set-up seems more like a dream - a dream of the easy life in a pleasant tropical backwater. Almost a survival from the past, you might say."

"Exactly, Pook, but speaking of the present, what do you see ahead?"

Peering at the skyline on the western horizon as it is dimly lit by the rising sun behind us, my binoculars make out a low hazy coastline some two miles in length. "India for sure!" I exclaim, hoping above all that it is not Cape Madalla. I couldn't go through that again.

"India! - only a couple of miles long and right out in the Bay of Bengal - impossible! It's an island."

"Then it must be the Andamans, sir. Stand by to go about."

"You certain it's not the Isle of Wight, Pook? The Andamans indeed! - where's your sense of direction? And in the name of all that's sacred at sea don't keep repeating the only order you seem to know, 'Stand by to go about,' or you'll drive me over the side. There must be another one you can learn before we perish. That land up for'ard just isn't marked on the chart, that's for sure. Get below and tell Honners the Astrologer I want him up here on the bridge dead or alive so we can find out what he's mucked up this time."

"Aye aye, sir." Despite the howling storm I spring to attention and salute smartly as though it was Navy Week in port, just to show Bray what kind of an officer I am under any conditions. Typical of his breed he spits to leeward.

Telling Honners is one thing but getting him mobile is another. He is lying spread-eagled on the deck as though he has lately fallen from the mast-head. "Don't bother the dying with stupid questions," he groans. "I've plotted the course on the chart and as far as I'm concerned you can dump me off anywhere along it, wrapped in a Union Jack."

"But the skipper wants you on the bridge at once, Honners."

My friend musters all his strength and sneers with it. "Tell that big ape that most of me is in the scuppers and what's left can't stir. I'm a goner, Peter, so let me spend my last hours in peace till the dreaded Ezooti claims yet another victim. . . . You stupid heartless cow!"

His outcry is occasioned by my lifting him up from the deck

like a babe in a shawl and carrying him to the bridge. He lies in my arms too enfeebled to protest anymore. Commander Bray eyes him with utter distaste written across his rugged features.

"Come here, Sagittarius, and point your little arrow at that lump o' vegetation up for'ard yonder. What do you make of it?"

Honners scans the heaving horizon with hopeless revulsion, but when he sees the island his face gives a hint of life.

"Land - beautiful land!" he whimpers. "Whatever the place is, just throw me on it. Anything to get off this switchback and lie down on something stable."

"I don't expect that kind of unprofessional cackle from my Navigating Officer, Honners," Commander Bray raps. "Pull yourself together, man, and let's recheck and take fresh sights."

Honners looks as if he is going to cry. "Have a heart, skippy, I'm all in. If you were a normal human being you'd know what it feels like trying to exist without a stomach."

Commander Bray blazes up. "For the last time, Honners, if you ever call me skippy again I'll see you're dismissed the Service. I demand to know what our exact position is, and the name of that island - got it? I stand on this bridge like a lost soul trying to obtain salvation while you act the kid, and if I ring down to the engine-room all I hear are the groans of Lieutenant Kala and his bolloo merchants waiting for the end of the world. Even the Gondah is too sick to shamble for'ard and squander our rice ration over the bows. As far as I'm concerned it's high time this cockeyed Navy ended its commission."

"You've still got me, sir," I remind him. "I'm standing to at action stations as usual, sir, ever ready to carry out orders in the best tradition of our Service, sir. You think up some command and I'm your man for turning to with all hands, sir."

I salute him smartly just to prove the old discipline is still alive. "Shouldn't we jettison stores or something, sir? Put out a sea-anchor, sir? Pump oil on the sea to windward, sir? You name it and I'll get activated, sir."

"The Andamans - or the Maldives, sir," Honners gasps, desperately searching his mind for island data.

"Or Iceland, eh, Honners?" Bray sneers disgustedly. "Once I beat round Cape Horn with a bunch of Lascars who'd put you to shame. Lie down on the deck again and shut up - that's about all you're fit for."

Ever on the watch, I shout anxiously, "Island coming up fast, sir. Let's clear it and identify it afterwards. Left hand down on the helm and hard a'port, sir."

Commander Bray leaps to the rail to sum up the position. "Too true, Pook. With this lot blowing we have no option but to beat round the southern extremity - or else we're in dead trouble. What a predicament to be in and break a sailor's spirit. Navigating Officer prostrate at your feet because there's a swell on; don't know where we are; can't identify a flaming great island; can't even find it on the chart. No wonder all his family were in the Army. God knows what they did when they came to a river. Probably had to dam it and walk across."

"I'll have you know we Pilkington-Goldbergs crossed the Rhine on horse...."

"Lie low, you useless ullage and pipe down."

Even as we scud sou'west towards the southern tip of the island it is obviously going to be close work to clear safely.

I scan the white shore for signs of life but nothing shows itself. Commander Bray personally takes the wheel from the quartermaster and gazes so intently to starboard that a picture of the Madalla Coast enters my mind with all its implications. It is dismissed by a curt order from our skipper.

"We'll clear the island all right, Pook, but get for'ard with the lead-line and take soundings just to be on the safe side - it may be a close shave. According to the charts there's nothing in this area less than fifty fathoms, but on the other hand they don't allow for any islands."

"Aye aye, sir, at the double," I rap back in the curt parlance of emergency, clicking my heels together and saluting like a robot. "Over the foc'sle in a flash, sir, sending back the required information essential to save the ship. Between us we can do it, sir, working as a team trained to the minute. . . . "

"Then for good luck's sake get for'ard and do it - and cut out the saluting every time you open your mouth. This is a crisis, not Visitors' Day."

"Message received, sir. There's only one question I must. . . . "

Commander Bray turns on me angrily so I depart on this vital assignment at full speed without receiving an answer to my inquiry, in the hope that I shall be able to lay my hands on a lead-line wherever one is supposed to heave it. Working on the assumption that there will be some information to bawl back to the bridge I grab a megaphone *en route.*

Once on the fore-peak I scurry around searching for the lead with the urgency of a lost ant, but it is just as I observe how close we are passing the island abeam that I have my first hallucination. Something appears momentarily above the waves and then disappears again. It is greyish in colour and quite smooth, like the back of a whale - not a cable's distance from the *Soonong*. Suddenly I spot another one, then another.

Forgetting all about the lead I stare over the rail hypnotized by these strange creatures. I sight seven in as many seconds, losing count eventually because the sea to starboard seems full of them. Momentarily I shudder as the thought of being wrecked amid these enormous beasts hits me. This horrible reverie is disturbed by urgent shouts from the bridge demanding instant information about soundings.

"Whales, sir," I bellow through the megaphone and saluting automatically. "Whales on the starboard bow - over there on the right."

"What's that you're hailing, Pook? How deep?" comes the reply above the wind.

"Whales, sir. A school of whales on the starboard whatnot."

Then I catch a glimpse of Commander Bray's florid outline on the bridge. It is mostly cap and mouth as he roars back, "Heave the lead, Pook - take soundings or all is lost - give me a depth for G . . . ."

In mid-sentence it happens. The ship suddenly creaks to a standstill, groaning from stem to stern, flinging me over the bow, megaphone and all. I plummet downwards, hit the waves, and then stand up idiotically as though it is a well-rehearsed stunt. Terror grips me to realize I am standing on the back of a mighty denizen of the ocean - so much so that I am rooted to the spot.

Commander Bray rushes for'ard to the rail with a lifebelt and rope at the ready, and looks down over the side. "You all right, Pook?" he shouts.

"Heave me the line fast, sir - the ship's rammed a whale," I explain at the top of my voice, yet without a trace of panic.

"Rammed a whale? What in hell are you on about, Pook? We've run aground on a sandbank."

"I thought it was a whale, sir," I admit frankly, glad nevertheless to know I am standing on a sandbank. "All the same, we were lucky not to hit one of those monsters - there's a school of them on the starboard beam between us and the island."

Commander Bray's eyes slit in his weatherbeaten face. "You got the gall to stand there on a dirty great sandbank and talk to me about whales in the Bay of Bengal, Pook? You mean to say you can't tell off-shore shoals from a school of whales? No wonder you were leaning over the rail, shouting out about whales when you should have been heaving the lead so we could clear the sandbanks. Still, I'm the biggest fool to waste time arguing with you - here you are, catch this line and swarm aboard before you get washed away, Nanook of the Polar Seas."

There is no denying that what would be a perfectly natural mistake on the part of a layman is very embarrassing to a Naval officer in my position. I try to discuss the matter with Honners but he looks away with a supercilious expression and utters a rude word. In my heart I know that he too thought they were whales, but he is so sore at being delayed on the journey that he won't admit it. The Gondah passes us in contemptuous silence, spitting betel juice on the deck with the force of an airgun. Commander Bray's face is so black that I feel duty bound to try and cheer him up. "Take heart, shipmate," I tell him reassuringly, "your matchless skill and daring will find a way to refloat the old *Soonong* on the flood tide - come rain, come shine."

"This is the flood tide," he grunts emotionlessly.

One cannot but notice an air of despondency hanging over the ship, yet no doubt you will agree that these are the very conditions under which true leadership proves itself. Thus I am spurred to point cheerfully to starboard and say, "This must be our lucky day, fellows. Just look at that beautiful island. Have you noticed something very strange about it?"

"As a matter of fact, I have, Pook - it ain't a whale," Bray rasps bitterly, "and doubtless a man with your keen powers of observation has already noticed that it's an island surrounded by water."

"Even stranger than that, sir. Look closely."

My enthusiasm puts new life into my fellow-officers who all peer to starboard in an effort to spot what I have seen.

"Give up?" I inquire triumphantly.

THIRTEEN

"All right, Pook, so we give up - but remember this is a matter of life and death, not a blessed quiz, so don't you dare tell me it's a naked woman camouflaged against the sand.

Whatever it is, you'd better make it good," Commander Bray warns me.

"Very well, sir. With that perspicuity one would expect of a true seaman I have observed that there is only one island."

Commander Bray tilts his head to one side and looks at me solemnly. "Brilliant deduction, Pook. Typical, if I may say so, and what one would expect when the village idiot is drafted to one's ship dressed as a lieutenant. Fancy that, only one island - and here's stupid old me thinking there were lots of them dotted about like whales. Hear that, Honners? - that island over there is only one, not several. Maybe we ought to ask Pook how many ships we're stranded on right now, eh?"

"Ah, sir, you're laughing at me, aren't you? I've made the old mistake of talking over your head, so let me come down to your level. I see it this way - every island I know in the Indian Ocean is always one of a group, usually a ring of little islands forming an atoll with a lagoon in the centre, like the Maldives. Yet here we have a solitary island in mid-ocean."

"So what does that prove, Pook? That this isn't the Indian Ocean? Surely you're not wet enough to dispute that?"

"Oh, no, sir, but you must admit it's strange. I'll work on it."

"Please yourself but don't let it dominate your life. Think about it while you're humping stores ashore."

It is surprising how quickly Honners recovers when he finds that we can walk to the island at low tide without so much as wet feet. The *Soonong* is high and dry on what is in reality part of the island, but her hold is a sorry sight where the shock of grounding has opened the hull plates. Commander Bray orders a camp to be set up on the highest part of the island, which is barely seven feet above sea-level, and all hands turn to for the transfer of stores to our new home. The place is about two miles long, four hundred yards wide and uninhabited, being a mere blister of sand sparsely vegetated by bushes. There are no trees which are so characteristic of coral islands.

Meanwhile Commander Bray makes no bones about breaking radio silence. He calls up Vizagapatam at the first opportunity, whereupon the following conversation takes place with the Chief Salvage Officer of the port.

"I'm aground 214 miles due east of Coconada, sir."

"You're what? Aground out in the Bay of Bengal? Isn't that rather difficult unless your ship draws 40 fathoms, Bray? You usually beach right here on the Golconda Coast where it's nice and shallow. We had you recently, remember?"

"I'm telling you there's an unidentified island out here - and I'm on it, high and dry. To be exact, my position is 17.41 North - 85.36 East. The *Soonong* is rapidly breaking up so I'm staying ashore till you come out and take us off."

"That's not going to be easy, Bray - the Japs are reported south of the Andamans. Nevertheless it must be done, so let's hope we can have you off in about 72 hours from now."

"That's the best news I've heard this month, sir."

"By the way, is the anchor safe, Commander Bray?"

"It is indeed - but how come you know about it, sir?"

"We were alerted this forenoon by C.S.O. Calcutta. Apparently the Nawab of Ramsam, plus a large party of top brass and camp-followers managed to escape the Jap push and decamped via Assam. At the moment they are recuperating at Dacca prior to reaching Calcutta. The Nawab sent you a personal message to ensure the safety of the anchor and other unspecified items you are carrying. He referred to the latter as eleven cases of groceries."

This wonderful news of our friends revives us as nothing else could, despite the sparsity of details, so we make the best of our plight and set to work for the purpose of sitting out the time under as comfortable conditions as possible. Commander Bray takes the precaution of burying the eleven chests well down in the sand lest we attract the attention of the Japanese Fleet.

The Gondah has been behaving strangely. He spends most of his time walking round the island in prayer, occasionally sniffing the air like an alcoholic passing a brewery. Eventually he comes to us across the sands in a very agitated state, accompanied by Petty Officer Zalu who acts as interpreter.

"Gondah says we standing on very sacred island, Sahib - Gondah says this is Pijee's Stepping-Stone, Sahib," Zalu informs us.

Commander Bray is in no mood for a revival of religious lore at the moment, and says so. "Tell him that's all over now, Zalu. The best we can do is wait to be picked up by our friends across the sea in India. Poor old Ramsam is kaput - finished."

"Gondah says this is treasure island, Sahib. Gondah says Astrologer Honners Sahib has been guided here by Pijee, Sahib. Gondah says. . . . "

"Your Gondah seems to have an awful lot to say considering I never see him open his mouth to a soul," I cut in. The only acknowledgement he has ever given me is a toothy leer every time

I make one of those small slips inevitable in the hazards of war, so that more than once I have been tempted to forget his robe of office and let him have it flush on his caste-mark."

"Gondah says *Soonong* is doomed as punishment for Pook Sahib losing chest in wreck," Zalu continues. First I was blamed for not finding the twelfth chest, but now it seems I actually lost the thing. Apparently the Gondah has the lot of us card-indexed.

I follow up with, "Well, Zalu, if your Gondah knows so much, why doesn't he tell us the name of this tight little island?"

"Gondah says this place is called Nagar Kutupos Island, Sahib."

"Rubbish. That's the island the Ramsamis tried to ship their valuables to back in 1824 - when the galleon foundered *en route*. Nagar Kutupos subsided below the ocean at the turn of the century and now it's not even marked on the chart."

Zalu smiles broadly. "Gondah says it is marked on his chakka, Sahib."

"Then let's have a shufti at his chakka right now."

The Gondah produces a dirty scroll from under his robes, spreading it out on the sand for all to examine. It is the tattered and patched remains of an Admiralty chart dated 1897, with the Nagar Kutupos Island carefully ringed round with a charcoal line. Honners checks the bearings of the island and confirms that they coincide with our present position, whereupon a long silence falls on the company.

Commander Bray is the first to speak, obviously in thoughtful mood. "It must be one of those islands which arise and subside over long periods of time. I've often heard about them but never actually encountered one till now. They tell me they are fairly common in this part of the world, though nobody really knows how it happens. Interesting, to say the least."

"I told you it was a strange island, sir," I remind him, "but as for us running into it - sheer coincidence."

"Gondah says it is the will of Pijee, Sahib," Zalu explains patiently. "Gondah says time has gone full circle and now treasure has reached destination."

We all think this is mere priest-talk but no one says anything. There is nothing much to say when you can't provide a better answer. Commander Bray again breaks the awkward silence. "Maybe there's more to this Pijee business than meets the eye, eh, Pook?" he muses.

I nod agreement. "Always thought there was, sir. We British are just kids when it comes to the occult, but I suppose we must be content with being the finest seamen the world has ever seen. No one can do the lot. Every man a master of his own craft, that's my motto - I'm a diver, not a diviner."

"So long as you're not claiming to be a seaman we'll let it go at that, Pook. Anyway, I hope we can bank on Pijee to keep up the good work by maintaining this little sandy platform waterborne and ensuring we get taken off in quick time. I'm certainly looking forward to seeing Rana again if she managed to leave Ramsam."

"Gondah says all will be well, Sahib," Zalu affirms happily.

"Gondah says Pijee always protect his own treasure, so send ship soon."

"You're positive of that, Zalu?"

"Gondah say so, Sahib, and who is doubting the Gondah?"

Nobody. From Commander Bray to lowly Bundi, all ranks have complete confidence in our new leader. So much so that if the Japanese Fleet were to appear over the horizon and engage us, we would take it on with supreme confidence born of the knowledge that defeat would be impossible. Nevertheless, it gives me an eerie feeling to hear Commander Bray consulting Petty Officer Zalu every eight hours or so, in the following terms:

"Stand easy, Zalu. How far off is the rescue vessel now, laddie?"

"Gondah says very near, Sahib. Roughly same distance as Shaggapore from Chattoo, Sahib. Gondah says very fine ship coming, Sahib. Arriving tomorrow, Sahib."

Even more unnerving is Bray's reply. "Message received, Zalu. Report again at dawn. If only they had a Gondah on board we could overcome the handicap of maintaining radio silence and find out what fresh news has come through from the Nawab."

"Gondah says Nawab in good health, Sahib. Gondah says Nawab very happy to hear groceries safe, Sahib."

"Splendid, Zalu, splendid- What did he say about the anchor?"

"Nawab say anchor fetch five rupees in scrap market, Sahib."

Commander Bray looks amazed at this turn of events. "But I thought the sacred anchor meant everything to you folks, Zalu. Just look at what we've all been through in- order to find it."

Zalu shrugs his shoulders in typical Ramsami pose. "Gondah says everything different now, Sahib. Gondah says remember ancient Ramsami wedding adage, Sahib: 'When tiger climb in bedroom, honeymoon begin in earnest'."

"Ah, exactly, Zalu. The Whole situation in a nutshell, one may say. Couldn't sum it up better myself."

I don't comment but my eyes go hard and my soul rebels to hear such nonsense, especially now that Bray of all people has fallen for this primitive mumbo-jumbo. There is scant consolation in knowing that I am the only sane person left in the whole company.

Honners is utterly lost, strutting about the island with a chart in one hand and Gipsy Martello's Almanac in the other, fully believing that he is a master of navigation by astrology. It is not pleasant to be stranded on this tiny island with a bunch of zombies.

Believe me, I never saw a more welcome sight than the

silhouette of H.M.I.S. *Bhavati* on the horizon at sunset the following evening as she cuts through the water from the west. To me it is like waking from a a bad dream to discover all is well once more. By the time she stands off the island and lowers her boats it is dark enough to see the constellation we call the Great Bear planted on the northern rim of the ocean like a silent sentinel watching over the rescue.

Looking up at it in a thoughtful frame of mind I think how remarkably like a bower-anchor it appears tonight, but quickly put such notions out of range by concentrating on the nearby frigate lying offshore which has been dispatched so expeditiously by the Royal Indian Navy for our succour. Then I dwell on Tina and smile happily. Only a matter of hours and we shall meet once more, I tell myself, taking a dirty piece of paper from my pocket which Zalu brought me earlier in the day and reading it yet again by the light of the moon. It bears the words I already know by heart: "Gondah says Tina awaits you at Vizagapatam and sends you message in ancient Ramsami adage - *When lovers reunited, snow melt on Himalayas.*"

Who wants it plainer than that? Leering almost evilly I re-fold my very own chakka and tuck it away safely. Then, hastily ramming on my cap to stop the moon beating down on my head, I hurry off to welcome the first cutter from H.M.I.S. *Bhavati*.

THE END